PIPE DREAMS

Jen LiMarzi

Copyright © 2025 Jen LiMarzi

All rights reserved

The characters and events portrayed in this book are fictitious. Any similarity to real persons, living or dead, is coincidental and not intended by the author.

No part of this book may be reproduced, or stored in a retrieval system, or transmitted in any form or by any means, electronic, mechanical, photocopying, recording, or otherwise, without express written permission of the publisher.

"I was really gonna be something by the age of 23..."
-Lelaina Pierce, Reality Bites

ONE

Half-dressed and half awake, I log onto my work computer at 10:15 from my Chicago home office, otherwise known as my kitchen counter. I'd moved into a tiny studio apartment three months ago during the finalization of my divorce and had yet to unpack much of anything beyond my espresso maker and what appears to be the rattiest of my clothes. Having overslept, yet again, I'm over an hour late for work at Reed, a college textbook publisher.

Twelve Microsoft Teams alerts and 34 e-mail notifications greet me upon signing on, which I address by scrolling through, rolling my eyes, and mouthing "I don't care." I align emoji reactions generationally with message recipients, sending hearts to the Gen Zs, priority exclamation points to the Millennials, thumbs up to the Boomers, and a few eye rolls and raised eyebrows to my fellow Gen Xers.

Within the last 15 years, my work environment has transformed into a modern adaptation of the movie *Office Space*. Last week we were told to replace our corporate headshots with avatars so that those employees who objected to having actual photos of themselves visible as thumbnails wouldn't feel uncomfortable or singled out. In addition to turning myself into a cartoon that day, I spent the rest of it messaging with Liz, my closest work friend who has weathered as many corporate changes as I have. We speculated that the company would be asking us all to wear ski masks at the next in-person corporate retreat.

When my work icon reveals that I'm online, Matilda, my seventh boss in the last two years, messages me with the always jarring "Chat?" Before replying, I take a quick peek at her public online calendar to see if she had any private or cryptically titled meetings this morning. It's my imperfect attempt to gauge if this call will be a legitimate check-in versus the catastrophized discussion I always assume it will be. With the number of layoffs and reorganizations that have happened at the company in recent years, I find myself spending nearly as much time snooping on the leadership team's calendars as I do completing actual work.

I reluctantly confirm my availability and within seconds my video call icon comes to life. I answer the call and, with no time to look in a mirror, see my face pop up on screen framed by a halo of wild red and gray hair and notice a large coffee stain on my ancient Throwing Muses band t-shirt with a stretched-out neck. I'm so preoccupied looking at my unkempt self that it takes me several moments to realize that Matilda is joined by an unknown man in a separate video window.

"Hi Matilda," I start as I run my fingers pointlessly through my hair. "I apologize for looking like such a mess, I had an early start and haven't had a chance to freshen up. I didn't realize we'd have company." I nervously smile and try to hover my mouse over the man's name on the screen to figure out who he is and what he does at the company.

"Jackie, this is Marcus from Human Resources," she says solemnly.

"Uh oh," I laugh in a panicked coping mechanism sort of way. I feel my chest start to tighten and my voice involuntarily shake. "Are we having another reorganization? I'm happy to discuss how my skillset can be of value in other areas of the…"

"Jackie," Matilda interrupts, "you have been a valuable employee for the better part of 15 years." Matilda's eyes are moving from side to side, clearly reading from a script on her monitor. "While we appreciate your time, efforts, and talents, the company has decided to go in a different direction, one that involves eliminating your position. Today will be your last day. I am unable to answer any specific questions related to your job or performance at this time, but wish you the best in whatever comes next." Matilda's screen goes black and Marcus' face fills the remaining space.

"I think we lost Matilda," I croak, while staring at Marcus.

"No, Jackie," Marcus corrects. "Per company policy, Matilda had to exit the call. I will now provide you with information on what comes next. Following this call your computer access will be terminated. You can bring your computer to any shipping location and once we receive it back, funds for your last paycheck will be released. You will receive a severance package for three weeks' pay and the remainder of the month's health insurance, after that time you may choose to continue on the company health plan through the COBRA program. Details will be mailed to your home address."

"What the..." I trail off, struggling to complete my thought. "I've been here for 15 years. Is everyone getting laid off or just me?"

"Jackie, per company policy, I can't answer any more questions at this time and would appreciate you remain calm and don't use hostile language or an aggressive tone in addressing me," Marcus drones on.

"I'm not being hostile," I state slowly in an attempt to appear calm and in control. "I'm just confused as to why I'm getting laid off and you're not giving me information or context."

"As I said, information will be mailed to your home address…"

"You don't even have my home address!" I spit back. "I moved, because I got divorced," my voice shakes.

"As long as your mail is being appropriately forwarded, the packet should still get to you," Marcus is clearly getting annoyed that I'm not going quietly into the night. "We wish you the best of luck."

The call abruptly ends. As soon as Marcus hangs up, my screen goes blue with a log on name that is not my own filling the space normally occupied by my credentials. I'm utterly confused.

I sit staring into the blue screen awaiting some sort of written directive or message to pop up more explicitly explaining what to do next as whatever Marcus told me mere minutes ago has left my brain. I'm supposed to mail this computer somewhere? What did he say? I feel numb akin to the combined shame, shock, fear, and confusion that gripped me last year when Dan confessed that he wanted a divorce.

My job was far from the dream career path in the art world that I'd imagined myself having when I graduated college with an art history degree years ago. But it was a much-needed paycheck and had been the one constant in my life for over a decade. Like many people, I've fantasized about quitting in a dramatic manner and telling everyone to go to hell as I move off to some bigger, better job, or buy a private island with random lottery winnings, but those workday fantasies were always on my terms. This reality is the complete opposite. I sit totally frozen for far too long trying to process what's happened. I simultaneously want to call my sister to tell her but fear the moment I do that it will become really real.

My phone starts to buzz with a text alert and I jolt out of my grief-filled stupor.

> Liz: What the fuck?! Are you OK? They just sent out a team e-mail saying you are no longer with the company. The wording and tone of it is making everyone question whether you quit, got laid off, fired, or died! I'm in the office today and the goons are roaming around pretending to make sure everyone is OK. We have a mandatory mindful session now scheduled for this afternoon.

> Me: I'm still alive – at least I think I am. I got the axe and was told the department was going in a different direction. 3 weeks severance, after 15 years! Brutal. Any idea if I was the only one? They wouldn't answer any questions.

Liz: I'm so sorry! As far as I can tell it's only you from our department, but they only e-mail to notify us about people we regularly work with. So maybe others from other departments?

Me: I'm sure my salary will really buoy the company bottom line.

Liz: Hang in there, my friend. I'll call you later and ask around to see if anyone knows what happened or about other positions at competitors where you can apply. Fuck this place, you deserve better.

Me: Thanks

Panic replaces inertia. I haven't updated my resume in 15 years. In fact, I'm not even sure if I have an old version on my current computer. How does a 52-year-old-woman who always thought of her job as an afterthought even get a job?

During my divorce, my attorney urged me to fight for more money from Dan, but apathy took over and I told her to back off. She warned me that a woman of my age with little savings and only enough retirement planning to be able to buy a cup of coffee couldn't afford to leave money on the table. While huge pieces of me wanted to fight for every dime he had to make him and his new soon-to-be wife as uncomfortable as possible, my pride and ego won out. I thought that telling Dan to keep his money and even take our crappy car, which was more of an albatross than an asset, would prove some sort of invisible point that I didn't need him and frankly never did. Though by his reaction, and my time now spent on public transit rethinking my actions, I'm pretty sure my decision was interpreted by him more as relief than self-reliance.

My mind swirling, I spin around to get a cup of coffee and knock over a nearly full glass of water. I freeze and watch in horror as a pint of liquid streams into the keyboard of the computer that is the key to my final paycheck. I open my mouth to scream, but no sound comes out. I scan the kitchen for something to mop up the liquid and an empty carboard paper towel tube sits on the counter mocking me. I take off my stained t-shirt and fruitlessly begin dabbing and mopping the water in hopes that this isn't a severance killing calamity, but knowing full well I have likely just bricked the computer.

My phone rings and as tears involuntarily stream down my face, I pick up Facetime with my sister, Debbie.

"Ewww, who answers a video call just wearing a bra? Your coworkers must love you," she grimaces.

"I just got laid off," I choke back tears. "And I just

ruined the computer that I am supposed to ship back in order to get paid."

"What? Oh god. But you don't have any money!" she blurts.

"I KNOW that DEBBIE!!"

"Sorry sorry…Oh Jack," she pauses. "What do you need? What can I do?"

Despite being my baby sister, Debbie was a grown-up long before I was remotely considered one. She was born overqualified to be a mother, caretaker, partner, badass, and "good girl" all in one. On top of it she is pretty and funny. This of course means that when I'm not totally enamored with her and thanking my lucky stars I have her as a sister, I kinda sorta hate her for being so perfect. Today, I need her more than anyone.

"I honestly don't know, Deb. I'm just, literally in shock." Tears continue to stream down my face as I stare at her staring at me in a stretched-out bra that ceased being an identifiable color roughly 500 washes ago.

"OK, here's what we're gonna do," she takes charge like she always does. "Ummmm…" I can literally see the wheels turning in her head in an attempt to think her way out of my disaster. "OK, yes. You're gonna take the day to process and I'll help, and then you'll move on. I mean you have no choice, right? On to bigger and better things," she says emphatically, as if stating something as if it is a fact will actually make it true. "Go take a shower, drink some coffee, put on presentable clothes, and come meet me and Maddy for lunch at 1:30. This will be perfect. I'm meeting her at the fancy restaurant in RH, you know, the old Restoration Hardware, and she would love to see you. And we can all hash this out over mimosas and overpriced fries."

My niece Maddy is 23 and has been earning mid six figures since she dropped out of community college two years ago. A social media marketing wunderkind, she somehow made herself into a lifestyle influencer and has already achieved a level of success that I can't fathom at more than twice her age.

"Why are you meeting her at a furniture store for lunch?" I ask, confused and still wiping away tears.

"It's a bougie furniture store that has this really lovely restaurant in the middle. It's just what you need. My treat. Maddy has to make some content or something, I don't understand half of what she's talking about. She's doing that first and then I think she might be ordering a couch for her new place. She sold her River North place and just bought this enormous loft in the West Loop and needs much bigger furniture to fill it up."

Hearing that my niece is juggling real estate deals and buying pieces of furniture that likely cost more than the final paycheck I may have just killed with a glass of water isn't helping me feel warm and fuzzy inside.

"I don't know, Deb," I sigh, trying to get out of having to leave the house. "I don't know that I'm up for hanging around a bunch of rich people in the state I'm in. I think I just need to sit and think for a bit and try to figure out my next move."

"Jackie, trust me, you have to get out of the house. I know you. We will figure this out together. If you don't come, you're just going to sit there all-day spiraling, then you'll start Googling Dan, open up a bottle of something that you'll regret in a few hours, and the next thing I know you'll be calling me, slurring your words, weeping, quoting sad 90s movies and asking where did it all go wrong."

"Bitch," I half whisper.

"Truth," she corrects.

"Fine," I say. "I'll see you at 1:30."

I zone out for 45 minutes in the shower but am still unable to wash off the layer of grime that this morning's layoff has added to the filth accumulating on, in, and around me this past year. When I finally step out, I catch a glimpse of myself in the full-length mirror before I have chance to wrap a towel around my body. Fifteen pounds heavier than I was when Dan declared he wanted a divorce a year ago and the weight of the world adding to the Earth's gravitational pull, I grab two towels and wrap myself like a mummy so as not to accidentally see myself again.

Since I took so long in the shower, I'm now on the verge of running late to meet Debbie and Maddy. I throw on a black loose-fitting t-shirt dress, run some product through my hair, and dab on some concealer and red lipstick to try to look somewhat presentable. Out in the main room of my apartment, my laptop sits wrapped in the stained t-shirt and hugged in a random beach towel. Feeling rage and anxiety even looking at it, I throw the computer, towel and all, into an empty Amazon box and prepare to ship it off at the drop-off location on the corner after lunch.

I head out the door, putting on big sunglasses to hide any puffiness or signs that I've spent the morning teary eyed while losing my job and mind. The entrance to my L stop is flanked by a roving cast of neighborhood characters that range from people peddling churros and religious pamphlets to those asking for money and assistance.

"Jack-AYYYY" echoes toward me, reverberating under the tracks. It's Freddy, a man who has questionable housing and hygiene, and an unhealthy relationship with alcohol. He is an indiscernible age somewhere between a rough 40 and a looks-good-for 60. While my apartment is new to me, the neighborhood is not and Freddy and I have been acquainted for some time. Several years ago, I gave him an expensive bottle of wine I'd passive-aggressively stolen from Dan's cousin's house after he made inappropriate political comments at a holiday dinner. Since then, Freddy's asked me for money or booze at least once a week.

"Hey Freddy," I say in a rushed tone hoping that he gets the hint that today's not a day to chat.

"Where you goin' all dressed up, girl?" he says passively blocking my path to the station entrance.

"Sorry, Freddy, I'm late to meet my sister for lunch," I reply.

"Must be nice!" he says sarcastically. "Going out for a fancy lunch in the middle of the week."

"I lost my job today, Freddy," I say bitingly while making direct eye contact. "I'm going because it's a free lunch."

"All right, all right, no hard feelings baby." He pulls out a small flask from his back pocket. "You want something to take the edge off? I've been there."

I look down at the well-worn flask and nearly break down at the kind, albeit gross gesture. It hits me all at once that this is the first nice thing that a man has done for me in months, and I feel the need to choke back tears.

"Thanks Freddy, I'll pass, but I really gotta go." I step around him and start walking toward the station entrance.

"No problem baby," he says loudly. "And if your sister's paying order a couple lunches and drop one by to ole Freddy on your way home." He starts cackling.

Moments later I'm on a train that smells like weed, listening to at least three separate people scroll through their Instagram and TikTok feeds at full volume without headphones on. I pull out my phone and attempt to remember the password to my LinkedIn account that I haven't accessed in at least a year. My profile pops up with a pre-pandemic version of myself staring back at me, sporting bleached blonde hair smiling ear to ear completely unknowing what the future would turn my life into. The details of my profile were sparse as I'd basically joined to have access to the platform in order to do some light stalking on new employees who seemed to be coming in and out of the company and Dan's girlfriend.

Two minutes scrolling through LinkedIn, I close the app and realize that everyone I've ever known or worked with now has a high-powered title where they are deemed an expert. It's as if I'd been frozen in time and sat idle in my career while they went off and became high achieving adults. I also learned that all the jobs in my field are seeking entry level workers or robots that get paid half of what I was making. Finally, I realize, I'm fucked.

I hop off the L and sprint to the restaurant, and as I walk in, I spray myself with the emergency perfume that I keep in my bag since my clothes now smell like I spent the morning getting high instead of taking a *Silkwood* shower. When I walk into RH, I see my niece talking and filming herself walking down a staircase. She has her phone rigged up on some sort of hand-held device with a fuzzy mini boom mic coming off of it. I open my mouth to try to greet and embarrass her, but Debbie catches my eye and starts waving as if she'll tackle me if I speak.

"This is her sixth trip down that staircase," she whispers angrily. "If you want to eat lunch today, don't interrupt her."

"I still don't know what the hell she does or talks about," I say pointing to Maddy as I watch her skip back up the stairs to apparently re-record whatever she was just saying.

We walk over to a living room display out of earshot of Maddy and take a seat on a cream-colored couch larger than the main room of my studio apartment. I start touching a large, random bowl of moss sitting on the coffee table, until Debbie slaps my hand and holds up a price tag showing that the bowl costs more than a used car.

"This place is insane," she says. We turn and watch Maddy bound back up the stairs seemingly to do another take of whatever she was recording.

"Who would've thought that pretending to show your real life would take so much effort," I joke.

"I don't completely get it either," she says. "But she's supporting herself and is wealthier at 23 than either of us, so more power to her. I just wonder what will happen to all these kids when they get to be our age."

"Speaking of kids, how's Cameron doing?" I ask, trying to delay any talk of my life and disastrous morning as long as possible.

Cameron is Debbie's younger son who is slated to graduate high school in a few weeks. He's a sweet kid, but never fully came into his own. For years Debbie brought him to doctors, psychologists, therapists, and counsellors in hopes of finding a diagnosis for his brand of "different," but never landed on one that stuck. He didn't excel at school, socializing, sports, art, music, or show interest in anything that other kids gravitated to. As far as we could tell his favorite hobbies were feeding the family cat and sleeping. For years, Dan and I privately referred to him as "weird Cameron," though part of me related to him being directionless, unmotivated, and decidedly average.

"He's good, he's good," Debbie squeals in an octave higher than her normal speaking voice in hopes that the repetition and high soprano delivery would make it true. "Not sure what he's gonna do after graduation. I think part of him sees Maddy and thinks why should he do any type of school or get a regular job, given how well she's doing with the social media thing. I'm hoping he can get a volunteer position at an animal shelter or something to try to get a better sense of what he's interested in."

"Well, if he finds anything that pays a living wage and requires no qualifications tell him to let me know," I say, half-jokingly. "I'm in."

Before Debbie could say anything consoling, Maddy appears typing away frantically on her phone.

"Hey you," I exclaim. "How did the stair walking video turn out?"

"Hang on aunt Jack," she says without looking up. "I'm just uploading this to the cloud so that my editor can add it to the afternoon content drop."

"You employ an editor?" I ask, incredulously.

"She has an editor, an assistant, and someone else that I can't remember," Debbie answers for her as Maddy is physically present, but mentally twelve other places.

"Damn," I reply. "You should see my social media. I have a Facebook account from like 15 years ago that exclusively serves me memes from mom and uncle Gary, and an Instagram account that has a few pictures of penis latte art that I got my barista in Wicker Park to foam for me. I basically just use it to hate stalk Dan and his friends at this point."

"Aww," Maddy finally looks up at me as if I'm a pathetic lost child at the mall. "That's so sad, aunt

Jack."

Maddy's wearing a cream-colored sweatsuit that matches all the décor in the high-end furniture store, bright sneakers with 4-inch soles, and is dripping with gold jewelry. Her hair is cut into a shoulder length bob with artfully painted highlights and half curls the width of a curling iron hitting at her cheekbones. Her makeup is so thick that she looks like she's a drag performer attempting to hide a five o'clock shadow rather than a beautiful twenty-something that has nothing to cover up.

The hostess catches her eye from across the room and we are brought into the center restaurant which looks like it could be in a photograph in *Architectural Digest.* Debbie and I gawk at the greenery and fanciness of the interior as we start to sit down.

"Can we have that table over there?" Maddy asks the hostess. "The light is just a little better."

I shoot Debbie a glance that she seems fearful to return. In my entire life I don't think I've ever asked to move to a different table in a restaurant even if I was sat practically in the bathroom. Without batting an eye, the hostess picks up the menus she'd laid down and brings them to the other table suggesting she's accustomed to this kind of request.

"I blame you if they spit in our food," I wink and

nudge Maddy when we settle into our new seats.

"They don't do that aunt Jack," Maddy rolls her eyes as if I'm the most embarrassing person on the planet. "You're just like mom. Your whole generation is just afraid to do or ask for what you want, so you just take it and complain after the fact."

"Ouch," I snap back. "Well, we're sorta damned if we do, damned if we don't. I'd prefer to be this way than labelled a Karen."

"Mom, order me a rose spritz if they come back before I'm back?" Maddy says nonplussed. "I just want to get a few more interior shots before we eat." With that she gets up from the table to take selfies and shots of the restaurant as if she is a wedding photographer.

"She's such a hard worker," Debbie beams.

"Well, that's one term for it," I say sarcastically.

"Hey," Debbie ribs. "She's employed, you're not, maybe you can learn something from her." I bristle knowing that unfortunately she's right.

"What am I going to do, Debs? I mean I'm 52. Who the hell is gonna hire me. And if I can't find something, where the hell am I going to live? Between the divorce lawyer's fees, the deposit and rent on the new apartment, moving, and everything else I'm looking at like three months before I'm begging mom to let me move back into my old room. And just for the record, if you tell mom I got laid off I will murder you. She's still blaming me for my divorce, I can't handle the job blame game too."

"I'm not gonna tell mom," Debbie assures me. "But Jackie, how can you have no savings? I mean retirement isn't that far off, what did you plan to do?"

"I planned to be married to Dan for the rest of my life," I say, embarrassed as I hear the words leave my mouth. "I know that's not an answer, but to be honest I hadn't even thought about it. We just always sorta lived like everything would work out and the two of us somehow scraped by. If he hadn't hooked up with his rich young girlfriend, you'd likely be having to buy him lunch too. We just never thought much about money."

Maddy returns to the table and drops into the conversation mid-sentence.

"Are you talking about uncle Dan? That's crazy about him having a baby," she says. Debbie shoots her a murderous look from across the table which startles the usually defiant Maddy.

"What?" I ask slowly and deliberately.

"Maddy," Debbie chastises. "Jack, we just found out. That's why I was calling this morning, to tell you. But then you sprang the layoff thing on me and I completely changed gears. Dan replied to my save-the-date e-mail for Cameron's graduation party with a note letting us know that Anna is pregnant."

Dan met Anna in a running group for people training for their first marathon. Despite my best efforts to extract the truth, he never divulged if he became involved with her before or after he let me know it was over between us. Either way, mentally, I choose to envision her like a caricature of a homewrecking villain.

I throw up my hands in an exasperated manner not sure if I am angrier at Debbie for inviting my ex-husband to her son's graduation or that my ex-husband has apparently completely started his life over within a brand new *Choose Your Own Adventure* book, while my book of life was just thrown in the trash. As if reading my mind Debbie heads off my argument.

"We had to invite him Jack," she says. "He's been part of Cameron's life for the last 17 years. He's still family."

"And you never even wanted to have kids, aunt Jack," Maddy says trying to be helpful.

"But either did HE," I respond a little too loudly. "Or maybe he just didn't want to have them with me. Oh, that's just great. Fan-fucking-TAAASTIC."

"Do you need a little more time?" our waiter, Kyle, comes by to ask.

"I need to turn back time, Kyle," I reply

sarcastically.

Debbie puts her hand over my arm as she and Maddy proceed to order and order for me as I continue to have arguments with Dan, my work, myself, my parents, and anyone else I've ever encountered within the confines of my own head. I see Maddy and Debbie exchange the knowing glances that I usually exchange with them at family functions when we see my mother or some other relative going off the rails.

"It's not a competition, aunt Jackie," Maddy says and puts her phone face down on the table. "You and uncle Dan just grew apart."

"He's doing that thing that all men having mid-life crises do," Debbie adds. "Instead of a sports car and hair plugs, he met a younger woman who looks at him like he's this wise and talented dude because he knows things, mainly because he's been on the planet so much longer than her. It makes him feel special and in turn he agrees to have a baby that he'll be dropping off to college when he's in his SEVENTIES. You don't want Dan. You're just upset that Dan is doing something new."

"But you'll be doing something new soon enough, aunt Jack," Maddy adds supportively. "You'll get a new job, you have a new apartment, maybe you can start getting on the apps and find a new partner too."

I sigh, roll my eyes, and wish I had the level of

optimism of a 23-year-old.

"I just thought of something," Maddy adds. "What if I do a little content sub-storyline for the next month or two on some of my MadLove channels." She starts frantically typing on her phone again. "Yes, this could work. You let me give you a life makeover, resume, apartment décor, hair, makeup, clothes, dating, oh my God, this could be perfect. I could expand my audience to older people."

"Wait, wait, wait, let me get this straight, you want to be my life coach?" I laugh. "I love you to the moon and back, hon, but I don't think a 23-year-old who has inspirational phrases haphazardly tattooed on her arms, and never had a long-term relationship or full-time job is really qualified to help turn the big ole battleship of my life around."

Maddy's face turns from excited, to crushed, to defensive in the span of ten seconds. She appears akin to how she looked when she was seven and I had to inform her in the American Girl doll store that unfortunately I couldn't afford to buy her a doll that looked like a creepy clone, a matching outfit, and a day at the doll spa. I can tell she is about to start yelling back at me.

"OK, OK, OK, both of you calm down," Debbie interjects to defuse the situation. Our food arrives and we all instinctively put on fake smiles to appear like nothing is wrong to the server. Maddy stands up and starts photographing our food and drinks, moving various dishes around to ensure they get the best light and angles. "I think Maddy may have a point."

I move my hands in the air incredulously, motioning that a woman-child taking pictures of her lunch shouldn't be my best hope at a future.

"Hear me out Jack," Debbie continues. "I think you just need some fresh perspective. Clearly everything you've tried up to this point is no longer serving you. I know Maddy is young, but she's quite successful and in touch with how the world works now. I mean I don't know that you have to get a full makeover to look like a 23-year-old, but you yourself said all your bosses are more Maddy's age than yours at this point. A new set of eyes and ideas can't hurt, right?"

I feel like a drug addict who suddenly realizes that they are at their own intervention. My mind is scrambling and I need to find a way out of this at least for the moment.

"I love and appreciate you both, you know this," I start. "But seriously I need to process what's happened. I mean I just got laid off this morning. Gimme a few days, weeks, a month to get my shit together, write a resume, see what's out there before we start reinventing the wheel. Ok?" I touch both their arms hoping that my calmed tones and therapy-sounding language of processing kicks the can of middle-aged woman makeover down the road a bit.

They both nod their heads in agreement. However, the problem with close family is that they know your tricks and tells. I see Maddy glance at Debbie and can read the unsaid conversation that conveys "I'll be seeing her by the end of the month."

After lunch we roam around the store where Maddy takes pictures and talks to sales people about the various shades of cream and beige all their furniture comes in. On three separate occasions girls and young women come up to her, sheepishly, and tell her they are big fans and follow her. She graciously thanks them and chats for a moment before taking a picture where their faces look like mine would have if I'd run into Cyndi Lauper or Pat Benatar at their age.

"She's really that famous?" I lean into Debbie speaking in a whisper.

"I don't think we know the half of it," she responds. "She's wiser than her years. Or at least she's really good at pretending to be."

Before leaving the store, I head to the bathroom, which may be the nicest public restroom I'd ever been in. While washing my hands I take note of the large stacks of super absorbent paper hand towels dotting the space between the sinks. Reminded of my computer water debacle and lack of paper products at home, I slyly grab a stack and stick them in my bag.

"Aunt Jack, if you need some money to tide you over, just let me know." I look up to see Maddy standing in the mirror before me.

"I will, hon," I lie. I touch her arm clad in the most expensive feeling sweatsuit material I've ever felt.

We part ways, and I decide to get off at the L stop before my own to take a walk to clear my head while simultaneously avoiding another banter session with Freddy at my usual stop.

I walk by a bar where Dan and I had been regulars in our twenties and thirties. I check my watch and at 4:30 deem it close enough to quitting time to go in for a well-deserved afternoon cocktail and a bit of nostalgia. Dark, nearly empty, and surprisingly unchanged by time other than a digital jukebox replacing the old standard, I grab a seat at the end of the bar and order a vodka tonic. I resist the urge to scroll through my phone and instead zone out thinking about all the times I spent laughing, dancing, and crying in this very spot.

"Jackie?" a voice asks from behind me.

"Carrie?" I reply incredulously. Carrie and her boyfriend Jeff were bartenders here when we were regulars.

"I haven't seen you guys in like, what, 20 years? I thought you moved away." She puts a backpack down behind the bar and then swings around the front to give me a hug and sits next to me.

"Oh my gosh! Carrie, it's so good to see you. I think at some point we just got lazy and ended up drinking even closer to home," I laugh. "Though I should let you know that Dan and I are divorced. Happened a few months ago. He did the middle age man thing and met someone half his age and is now apparently having a baby with her." I tip my glass in the air.

"Oh wow," she says. The bartender comes by and puts a glass of seltzer water in front of her.

"What about you?" I ask. "I see you're still working here. Whatever happened to Jeff?"

"Jeff and I got married," she says. "Probably right around the time we lost touch. Ya, we got married, had a kid, and actually bought this place."

"What?" I look around the bar seeing it with different eyes. I'm hit with a wall of feelings that I can't quite place. I always assumed people I'd lost track of from my twenties who were wilder, more directionless, or expectation-less would have been stuck in the lives they held when they were 25. Hearing of Carrie's moving on beyond that version of herself instantly made me confused, envious, and like I'd missed the memo to become some version of an adult that even those no one expected to become successful had received.

"Yeah, the previous owners were retiring, so we decided to buy it from them. It's been great. The neighborhood has certainly changed a bit since then. There are million-dollar condos and houses and whatnot. But that honestly has been pretty good for business. Are you still living around here?"

"Ya, ya, I live a little bit closer to the California stop," I say. "But I met my sister and niece for lunch and just decided to take the scenic route home and thought I'd stop in for old times' sake."

"I'm so glad you did," she says. A small group of people stream in and take aim at a table in the back. "Are you staying for a bit? I just have to help Simon close out his shift and then I'll come back and catch up with you."

"Yeah, yeah, for sure," I respond. "I'm not going anywhere." She touches my back and gets behind the bar to work.

I pull out my phone to hide the fact that I feel lonely, old, and unaccomplished. I pretend I have some very important texts to respond to as I read my Google newsfeed about celebrity gossip, the best places to retire, and high protein meals to make right now.

Five vodka tonics and three hours later, I stumble out of the bar into the reality of the evening. I am unemployed, alone, need to walk home, and already have to pee.

TWO

I wake up with a splitting headache at 11:30 the next morning. While not a stranger to a boozy night out, five vodka tonics following a chalice of lunchtime mimosas has pushed my aging body to the limit. I feel like crap.

I grab my phone to see that I have a voicemail from Liz.

> "Hey Jackie, it's Liz. Just calling to check in on you and see how you're doing and give you the scoop here. From what I was able to gather, I think they got rid of at least five long-time employees who were in non-managerial roles within the editorial department. Basically, cleaning house of everyone over 50 who probably made living wages. There was a larger team town hall about cost cutting measures, innovation, blah blah. My guess is they are going to try to off-shore or use AI to cover everyone's roles. Assholes. Listen, you were

always too good for this place. I will keep my ear out for any jobs that come up out in the world, but let me know if there's anything else I can do. Chin up buttercup and try to enjoy this time off."

Liz's voicemail brought a sense of relief that I wasn't alone in being let go, but also a sense of melancholy. While Liz and I had worked together for years and trauma bonded over all the reorganizations and seemingly ridiculous corporate decisions made by higher ups, at the core, we were remote work friends with no in-person foundation. As much as I would like to think we will stay in touch and have the same relationship we always had, I know from past experiences that once that day-to-day commiserating is done, remote work friendships become relegated to an annual holiday e-mail or attempt on WhatsApp to have a virtual happy hour with the "old gang" where those no longer at the company pepper the one person still there for gossip and reassurance that they are better off elsewhere.

In thinking about this, I wonder if Maddy and her generational counterparts who have so many of their relationships solely online will eventually feel this sense of melancholy on a grander level. When they are in their early fifties will their existential crisis be less about what's the point of everything and more about how they have never had a real relationship with anyone?

With my head pounding and a tongue that feels like sandpaper I stop trying to solve generational emotional calamities and turn my attention to getting a glass of water, some food, and ibuprofen. Stepping around the half-wall of my alcove studio, I see that my combination kitchen and living room looks more like a fraternity flop house rather than a middle-aged woman's serenity palace. Half open boxes from never quite moving in are still strewn about covered with clothes, random framed photographs and books, along with objects that likely had no business moving with me, but I wasn't about to let them stay with Dan out of spite.

Our former apartment occupied the top floor of a vintage Greystone building in Wicker Park that was spacious if not a bit neglected. While it meant we had intermittent heat and low water pressure, it also meant we had an elderly landlord who rented it to us when the neighborhood was questionable at best and chose not to raise the rent even as the neighborhood gentrified. When his daughter became involved in his finances, our luck ran out in lock step with the lifespan of our marriage.

I chose to stay in the neighborhood out of inertia and ended up in a new construction tiny studio paying the same price as we did for our huge vintage three-bedroom apartment. Dan moved into his new girlfriend's Lincoln Square townhouse that I suspect is owned by her parents as her job seems to be wearing yoga pants, stealing husbands, and saying the word marketing now and then.

As I gulp down a glass of water, I notice a piece of paper has been slipped under the door.

> *Ceiling leak in the apartment below. Plumber coming between noon-2 on Friday to inspect your kitchen pipes. If you won't be home to let them in, call Junior. -Building Management*

Fantastic. Just what I need. I put a reminder on my phone and take a seat on the couch where I decide to treat and soothe my aching mind and body by watching an episode of a mind-numbing reality show about selling luxury real estate in California before I switch gears to start looking for a new career in earnest.

For the first hour, I watch with my mouth agape as a group of women who look like a combination of drag performers and "street walkers" as my mom would say, walk around an office in five-inch heels, mini-skirts, and crop tops being mean to each other talking about selling houses worth millions of dollars. Their skin is pulled taut, their lips are inflated, and their eyelashes look like something Jim Henson would have created for a Muppet. How do these people exist? And who would hire them to help navigate their largest monetary investment?

As the first episode ends with a group of women yelling at each other at a brokers' open, I find myself both laughing at the absurdity of this spectacle and needing to find out what happens in the next episode. I look at my watch and negotiate that watching one more episode won't impact my future, so I click next and settle down for hour two.

Two days later I have watched an interchangeable cast of real estate brokers sell homes up and down the California coast, while they have relationships and catfights that resemble the 80s shows *Dynasty* or *Dallas*. Unfortunately, I haven't so much as put together a current resume or applied to a single job. As Netflix tells me I only have two episodes left in my current season of debauchery, I get a text.

> Fucknut Dan: Hey, we just got a Priority Mail envelope forwarded to our address. Anna had to sign for it and opened it because she didn't realize it was addressed to you. It's employment separation papers. Sorry. I'll be in the old neighborhood Friday morning for a dentist appointment, I can bring them and drop them off somewhere or just mail them. Let me know what you prefer.

While I haven't had a date in months, at least

I'm getting fucked in multiple other ways. I pause the TV and stare at the phone careful to not start typing as the appearing and disappearing dots would be a sure sign that I am giving this all way too much thought. I don't even know where to begin. Frozen in space and time I continue to stare at my phone until I just go numb. I then push play on the TV remote and continue to watch trashy realtors belittle each other in skimpy outfits.

As I notice it start getting dark outside, I realize I have become one with the couch and not gotten up in hours. I throw on a pair of leggings, an old Veruca Salt band t-shirt, and a hoody and decide to restock my supply of vodka and snacks at the Binny's down the block. As I grab my wallet and phone, I look down at the text from Dan still sitting on the screen like a time bomb. I finally reply.

> Me: I'll meet you in front of the dentist office at 10 am on Friday.

Within seconds I get the obligatory thumbs up emoji which inspires a double middle finger gesture from me standing in the kitchen.

Walking outside is jarring when you haven't left your couch in hours. I feel akin to how I did nearly a decade ago when my father was in hospice dying from glioblastoma. Debbie and I spent hours just sitting in his room awaiting the inevitable. Once it happened, I remember walking out of the building to her car genuinely shocked that things like weather, sunlight, conversations, and other people's lives had continued going on while mine seemingly had been frozen in that little dark room.

Realizing I hadn't showered in as many days as my new realtor friends had been incessantly peddling their wares, I quickened my pace until I was firmly inside the Binny's, afraid of who I might accidentally run into looking like a version of the Unabomber. Past the craft beers, artisanal sodas, small batch whiskeys, and celebratory displays of champagne, I grab a mid-sized bottle of vodka and bare bones tonic along with a large bag of pretzels. The line of customers ahead of me waiting to check out looks like a motley crew of early twentysomethings, trying on various identities while secretly proud of themselves for being able to buy alcohol without fake IDs. As I stand there judging them and attempting to figure out what their plans might be for the evening, I'm jolted into reality by the sound of my own name.

"Jack-AYYYY!!! I thought that was you, woman!" Freddy's deafening voice makes everyone standing in line turn around to stare. "You shop here too. All right all right, today's my lucky day."

"Hey, Freddy," I say with a somewhat apologetic tone. He's surveying all the smaller bottles of hard alcohol arranged in a display at the front of the store.

"Whatcha got there? Vodka and pretzels? Looks like someone's having a party," he laughs. "Maybe you pick me up a little consolation gift since it appears my invitation got lost in the mail?"

Security, the cashier, and all those within a three-aisle radius are staring at me, begging me with their eyes to please just buy this man whatever he wants so that their night doesn't have to start with a scene.

"One small bottle," I agree. "That's it. I lost my job, remember?" I mumble this last part recognizing that those words may change perceptions of me from being the middle-aged lady who enables the neighborhood alcoholic, to lumping us together as two down-on-their-luck neighborhood alcoholics.

"That's my girl!" he smiles revealing two missing teeth that I don't remember having been missing just a few days ago. "Do I want whiskey? Vodka? Ohhh Malort, that stuff is NASTY."

"Ok, Freddy," I try to de-escalate his public review of the entire display. "Pick something, let's get moving. I have to get home." He hands me a bottle of whiskey and then stands right next to me as I pay the cashier to ensure I don't walk away without giving him his selection.

"No need to put that one in a bag," he points to the cashier. "I'm environmental, I save the trees and plastic." He starts laughing hysterically at his own joke.

I hand him his parting gift and hope that he just takes it and leaves. Instead, he tags along next to me as we walk out the automatic doors. Freddy lights a cigarette and puts the bottle of whiskey in his back pocket.

"Do you have somewhere to sleep, Freddy?" I ask.

"Girl, you think I'm *that* cheap of a date? You buy me a fifth and I'm just gonna sleep with you?" Freddy let's out an infectious cackle that sounds like 30 years of cigarettes trying to escape his lungs. I roll my eyes. "Don't worry about me Jack-aay. I'm doing just fine. You're the one I'm worried about, moping around the hood like it's the end of the world. Life's too short for that. Hang in there baby-doll." He sees someone across the street that starts waving at him. He winks at me and jogs across the street weaving between moving cars before reaching his friend.

I return to my apartment, look at the bottle of vodka and think better of pouring myself a drink. Instead, I sit on the couch, crunching on pretzels, and scrolling through my phone. Both Debbie and Maddy have been texting daily to check in, but all I can muster are a few heart and thumbs up emojis in return. I look Maddy up on Instagram and watch a reel that she created the day we went to lunch. Her multiple trips up and down the staircase, posing with food, and roaming around the store was transformed into 25 seconds of "content" that made it look like she'd spent the day lounging in a cream-colored paradise totally engulfed in luxury. In that moment even I wanted to be her and by the thousands of comments and reactions I wasn't alone.

I quickly scroll through a few job boards and realize that when you can't even come up with a key word or category to type in to the job search bar, you probably have no business even applying to a job. My perusal of job sites has led to the mysterious algorithm serving me up articles with quizzes and flow charts to help me ignite my passions, find my true self, and get the career I've always wanted. I throw my phone to the other end of the couch and click on the TV to see what my real estate friends are up to.

By Friday morning, other than consuming hours of brain rotting "reality" content and pounds of body rotting processed foods, I've done little else. I have a nervous pit in my stomach, remembering that I have to meet Dan. I look in the mirror and see wild hair, a puffy face, and skin that looks like it hasn't seen the sun in months. I shower and use all the products in my bag of tricks to disguise what my life has become over the last few days. Instead of pulling on one of my 90s band t-shirts that are strewn about the apartment, I put on the t-shirt dress I wore to lunch with Debbie and Maddy in an attempt to look presentable without trying too hard.

I walk over to the dental building a few blocks away. Dan and I had back-to-back appointments there for years. In fact, right after we separated that was one of the first things I changed out of fear that the office staff might ask me where he is and send me into a tailspin.

From across the street, I see Dan getting out of a Mercedes SUV after parking in front of the office. He still looks and dresses like he's a missing member of the band Weezer, but since he started dating Anna his clothes and style have taken on a more expensive appearance. No longer is he wearing faded and dingey t-shirts that have been worn and washed 7,000 times. Instead, his semi-vintage-hipster style looks more purposeful and curated, like an artisan designer made his clothes look lived in versus time and tumult.

"Hey," I say as I approach. "Did you get rid of the old Honda?"

"We actually donated it," he replies. "Anna can't drive stick and said she wanted something newer and safer. Her dad's firm got us a good deal on this one." Instinctively, I make a tsk sound with my tongue, suddenly sympathizing with our old Honda that has been traded in for a newer shinier model.

"You said you didn't want the car," he responds to my reaction.

"I always hated finding parking, digging it out of the snow, and paying speed cam tickets. Plus, it's just more eco," I cover, trying to inject a dose of righteousness. "Doing my part to save the planet." He ignores my pathetic attempt at a dig.

"Hey," he replies. He hands me the thick priority envelope, ripped open on one side. "Sorry again about the mix up with opening it. And sorry about the job."

"Yeah, well," I reply. "I guess editors, and maybe even textbooks, have outlived their usefulness. But I have some other irons in the fire." Words tumble out of my mouth that have no business reaching the light of day.

"Oh," he says surprised. "That's good. Another editorial job?"

"I'm actually thinking about going into luxury real estate sales," I squeak. I regret it almost as soon as I say it. Despite no longer being a couple, Dan knows me inside and out. He can detect my lies way more easily than I can detect his.

"Really?" he asks with an odd smirk on his face.

"Ya," I continue, doubling down on my lie. "Been doing a lot of research and it's quite lucrative."

"Is watching twelve seasons of *Selling the OC, Selling Sunset,* Selling-other-places reality shows your research?" he laughs. When he sees the confusion on my face he says, "You're still using my Netflix account, Jackie. I honestly don't care, other than you're totally screwing up my algorithm." I'm mortified.

"Wow, so you're reading my mail, checking up on what I watch on TV, do you want me to install a camera in the apartment so you can see what I eat too?" I know I'm getting both defensive and offensive out of the shame of being caught in both a lie and for watching embarrassing television, but I can't stop myself.

"Geez," he says. "Calm down, I'm just joking with you."

"At least I'm not having a BABY!" I snap back in a way that angers even myself. He's caught off guard and his body language changes. "I didn't mean it like that," I soften. "It's just, when Debbie told me… I guess I really never knew you."

"It's not like that Jacks," he tries. "You know me, I never wanted kids. It wasn't planned. But when it happened, Anna explained that she always wanted kids and I thought, why the hell not."

"That's the rationale for trying a new restaurant or haircut, not bringing a person into the…" I trail off shaking my head, realizing his decisions no longer impact my life.

"Stop it," he scolds. "You know, it's not that I went off looking for someone else, Jackie. I just wanted to grow up and you seemed to have zero interest in that. Yeah, it was great to go out drinking or seeing bands we saw a million times over the years, or blow an entire paycheck on a trip somewhere. But I want to live like a grown up. Own a place, cook meals, care about my job, care about doing more than scrolling through my phone on the couch, not paying attention to the person sitting three feet away. You just seem to want it to be 1998 forever. And it's not! I'm not. We had a great time, but we just grew apart."

"And now you're picking up where I apparently left you stuck?" I dig back. "Gonna be the 55-year-old first time dad with your do over wife? Tick off home ownership and all of life's other milestones thanks to your girlfriend's parents?"

"Forget it," he shakes his head. "Why do I try? Look around Jackie, you're unemployed, living in a neighborhood where nearly everyone is half your age, paying God-knows-what for rent for the privilege of doing so, and wondering where it all went wrong. Time's running out. You need to look in the mirror and realize you're an adult. Pretending not to be one isn't doing you any favors."

"Thanks for the papers," I squawk. "I'll see you at Cam's graduation party in June. And good luck with the baby...you'll need it" My eyes well up with tears and I turn my head as I start walking away in hopes he can't see that he has stuck the reality knife in once again, this time very deeply.

"Jackie!" he calls back somewhat apologetically. I wave my hand and continue on my path forward, determined not to look back.

When I make it back to the apartment, I immediately sign out of Netflix and proceed to break down sobbing uncontrollably. I think all of my anger and rage toward Dan has superseded my ability to process the grief of the situation. I look around the apartment at the piles of 90s band t-shirts, the mess of boxes, the pretzels for dinner. I consider the state of my bank account and hear Dan's comments echo in my head as the truth. I'm 52 and in an effort not to become a "sell out" I've apparently wasted the last thirty years of my life.

When I begin to calm down, I slowly snap out of at least some of the stupors that have been hanging over me like a fog the last few days, weeks, and months. Both proving Dan right and attempting to prove him wrong I use the spirit of my 90s angst to push me forward. I take off my dress, throw on a Dinosaur Junior t-shirt and a pair of jean shorts, and play Liz Phair's *Exile in Guyville* album on the living room speakers. Partly dancing, partly singing along, I start to sift through the contents of the boxes that are strewn about trying to put them in some sort of order. I throw dirty dishes and mugs into the sink and consolidate several half-eaten bags of pretzels into one pretzel mélange in a bowl on the counter. After an hour, feeling accomplished, I look around and recognize that I've barely made a dent in the chaos and inertia that my apartment has become.

I hear a knock at the door and immediately steal myself for an altercation with a work-from-home neighbor who is probably on the other side of the door wanting to complain about the music and banging. I open it to find a tall man with an untamed mustache, roughly my age, carrying tools, and looking to push past me to get into my apartment.

"Can I help you?" I ask slightly perturbed.

"Oh, wait, do I have the right apartment?" he looks at his phone. "Are you Jaqueline Novak? I'm Brian from Windy City Waterworks. The plumbing company. I think your management company should have let you know we were coming. The downstairs neighbor has some staining on her ceiling that we have to investigate."

"Oh my God, right," I remember. "Come in. I'm sorry. I totally forgot."

"No problem, it looks like you have your hands full getting ready to move," he looks around at all the boxes and crap strewn about.

"Actually, I'm sorta unpacking from a move in," I laugh. "Well three months ago. It's been an interesting six months. Divorce, layoff, denial, breakdown. You know, life." I'm not sure why I feel the need to confess personal details of my life to this stranger.

"Ahh," he says setting his tools down in the kitchen. "I've been there." He gestures toward the kitchen cabinets under the sink to request permission to take a look. I nod back.

"I was about to make myself a latte, do you want one?" I ask. "The one thing I was able to salvage from the relationship and actually unpack is the fancy coffee maker."

"Sure, if it's not a lot of work," he replies. "I've been going since 4:30 this morning. Got an emergency call of a broken sump pump that was flooding these people's basement in North Center. The added fee is fantastic, but all things being equal, I think I would've preferred to sleep for the extra few hours."

Within minutes of sticking his head under the kitchen sink, he pulls out the dishwasher and puts it in the center of the kitchen to look behind it, inspecting the various hoses and adjacent pipes.

"I'm not seeing any pooling or staining," he observes. He stands up and knocks on the wall near the kitchen counter. I hand him the latte, which looks particularly undersized in his large hands. He takes a sip and foam gathers on his mustache. "This is really good. Do you work in a coffee shop?"

"At the rate I'm going, the answer will probably be yes," I sigh. "Though I must admit, going to coffee shops is probably my favorite activity at the moment."

"Well you should consider it," he says. "I'd buy this from you."

"Thanks," I add, considering whether or not to tell him he has milk foam on his face. "What's the verdict on the plumbing."

"I'm not exactly sure. These buildings get tricky. You know people get all excited about new construction, but give me an old building any day. Yeah, they're finicky, but those things are built to last. These developers cut corners, grease the palms with the permits, seal up the walls and you have no idea what's happening. Leak could be coming from somewhere in this wall, under the floor, or even from the people above you," he explains. He stops to take another sip of coffee and looks up and down again. He has a strong midwestern accent and forearms the size of small tree trunks. "Best bet, I think, is to open up the ceiling in the apartment below to try to see what we're dealing with and then trace it from there. She's not gonna be happy, but not sure there's any other way to do it."

"I don't even think I've met the downstairs neighbor," I confess. "Like I said it's been a whirlwind."

"You married a long time?" he asks. He's moved to the other side of the kitchen counter and is half leaning, half sitting on the bar stool. "I mean, it's none of my business, but that's one of the perks of the job. In exchange for rifling through people's hair clogs and sewage, I get to be nosy and chat with interesting people."

"Unfortunately, I don't think I'm all that interesting," I sigh. "But ya, we were married for about twenty-five years. I just found out that he's having a baby with his 27-year-old girlfriend."

"Ouch," Brian laughs. "Though I shouldn't talk. I've been divorced twice. First wife and I married almost straight out of high school, had two kids and by the time the kids hit middle school we were such different people that we were both glad to be rid of each other. We're friendly now, but it took a while. I have two great daughters though. Second wife, I kinda pulled what your ex did. Married someone much younger. I wasn't thinking with the head on top of my shoulders if you know what I mean. That one was a total disaster. She had daddy issues and anger issues. It only lasted two years and the divorce was a mess."

"Think you'll ever do it again?" I ask. "Get married? I mean not that it's any of my business, but that's one of the perks of living in a leaky apartment, I get to talk to interesting plumbers." I smirk and he returns it with a grin.

"I dunno," he says. "I'm 54. I'm not dead yet. So I never want to rule out anything. But I think when you get to be my age it's more about wanting to be around someone who gets you and makes you happy versus all that let's play house kinda stuff that seems so important when you're young. Maybe that includes marriage, maybe it just means finding a person you are perfectly happy doing nothing with."

"I'm 52, so I'm right there with you," I agree. "It's just all very daunting. Now everyone does the apps for dating and whatnot. I feel like a dinosaur."

"I'm kinda an old school guy," he replies. "I've tried them, don't get me wrong. I've swiped and all that. But you really meet some doozies on there. Half the time I'm not sure if they're real people. Though the few I've met in person turned out to be just as nuts as they were online. I'm kinda a friendly guy, so I prefer meeting people more *organically* as my daughters would say. You?"

"I've looked online," I confess. "But I kind of chicken out and then end up just Googling my ex and getting pissed off at him."

"You still in love with him?" he asks.

"NO!" I snap.

"Kids?" he adds.

"Nope," I reply.

"Then my advice, not that you're asking," he smirks, "get out there and move on. Whether that's dating or sleeping around, or just taking up a new hobby that has nothing to do with anything you ever did with him. He's moved on." He pauses and takes another long sip of coffee. "I saw my cousin get stuck in this anger thing where she spent years trying to punish her ex by showing him how miserable her life had become because of him. But he'd moved on and she wasted years just being angry and miserable, and he didn't even notice. You guys had your run, it was good while it lasted, I assume, and now is your chance to try something new."

"With a 52-year-old body," I laugh. He stands up and mock looks me up and down.

"Ain't nothing wrong with that body," he winks in a way that is endearing and not creepy. "It's just lived in and I'm guessing you know how to use it by now." Mildly flattered, we both laugh and stand in the kitchen awkwardly.

"Well, thanks for the therapy session," I joke.

"Thanks for the coffee," he replies while putting the empty mug on the counter. "Back to your plumbing. Do me a favor and don't use your dishwasher for the next couple of weeks while we get this sorted. Though by the looks of things," he gestures to the mountain of dishes in my sink, "I don't think that will be a problem."

"Heyyyyyy," I jest, knowing he's right.

"I'm gonna go talk to the neighbor now and try to get her on the schedule within the next two weeks to open up that ceiling and then once we see what's going on there I can let you know what, if anything, we have to do in your place."

"Sounds good," I say.

"All right Jackie," he smiles as he picks up his tools. He sticks out his hand and gives mine a squeeze and shake that is reassuring. "It's been a pleasure. Good luck with everything. Try to go out there and do something different and exciting," he laughs. "And ya, we'll be in touch about the pipes."

"Thanks, Brian," I reply sincerely. "I appreciate it."

He leaves and I feel a little glimmer of pride at my ability to successfully talk, and I dare say slightly flirt, with a man who isn't Dan. I turn around and look at my apartment through what I imagine to be this stranger's eyes. I see my mess and disorder and hear his words inspiring change reverberate in my head. I pull out my phone and decide to do something different.

> Me: Maddy...I've been thinking about it. If you'll still have me, let me be your life makeover content. I'm ready for something different and exciting.

THREE

On Monday morning I buzz myself into Maddy's apartment building in the West Loop with a feeling of nervousness that seems disproportionate for a grown woman visiting her niece. Maddy was thrilled when she heard that I was open to her intervention of sorts and asked that I come to her place to meet her team and plot out the course of my "content."

The old warehouse building, like most of those around it, had once been a site of manufacturing and industry. Today nearly all of the buildings in the area have been transformed into overpriced lofts within walking distance to restaurants and bars owned by famed chefs, mixologists, and prospectors. Debbie swooned when she talked about Maddy's apartment so I brace myself to be blown away.

"Aunt Jackie!!" she yells enthusiastically when she opens the door. "I'm so glad you're here." This is perplexing given that the last few times that I've met up with her, Maddy couldn't be bothered to look up from her phone for more than three minutes. I realize that the key to her heart is being the subject of content. "Come in, come in, let me give you the tour and introduce you to the team."

Debbie wasn't exaggerating when she said the place was impressive. It looks like one of those movie apartments that forces you to shout at the screen "how do you afford that place?" The main room is enormous and open with soaring concrete ceilings held up by columns and beams. The back wall is nearly all windows that lead out to a private rooftop deck. To the right a bedroom is visible behind a half open sliding barn door. At the other end, next to the industrial looking kitchen, is a long dining table that appears to double as mission control for Maddy's online enterprises. The table has three young people sitting around it clacking away on laptops and phones.

"Everyone," Maddy commands as she walks me toward the table. "This is Jackie, who will be featured in future content. She's the one I mentioned, who I think can help us expand our audience demographics. Jackie this is everyone." They all look up and give me a once-over glance that is simultaneously polite and judgmental. "This is Riff who uses they/them pronouns. They are my creative director and they are amazing at thinking out of the box. Arlo, he/him, is my editor and producer. He secures most of my sponsorship deals and cuts the longer form content. And then Janelle, she/they, is my assistant and keeper of all things schedule and is the key to my life."

"Wow," I say. "Quite the team." They all look at me non-plussed and I can see them exchanging somewhat quizzical looks amongst each other, likely wondering why they are suddenly branching out from overpriced couch content targeting affluent young people to trying to revamp the life of a 50-something-year-old woman who they probably see as the problem with the world.

"So," I say brightly and earnestly. "How will this all work? Are you doing a *Queer Eye* type thing? Like a bunch of people redo my apartment, get me a job, date, and new haircut? Or will it be more of a montage, kinda like that scene in *The Devil Wears Prada*, where Stanley Tucci turns Anne Hathaway into a glamorous *Runway* employee?"

"Aww," Riff says, "she's so cute. She kinda reminds me of my mom." He puts his head back down and starts clacking away on his laptop. Confused, my face visibly falls as I wonder what I have actually committed to being part of.

"Aunt Jackie," Maddy says, "I think you're going to be a bit more like a feature on some of my short form content. So think less of a *Queer Eye* episode and more of a few Instagram Reels or maybe a TikTok...well hmm...I don't know if you'll get traction there. Riff?" Riff shakes their head no without taking their eyes off their computer. "Ya, so Instagram, maybe a few YouTube shorts. Just showcasing some brands that I've not worked with before and expanding the breadth and type of content I work on to show range to other future sponsors."

"Oh," I try to hide my disappointment. "Right."

"Ya," Arlo speaks up. "So Maddy, I reached out to a bunch of sponsors that could work and there was definitely some interest. ZipRecruiter is interested in a sponsored piece on job hunting, we may have the Container Store related to an apartment revamp, Makeup Mecca is tentatively in, but likely would want you to promise a long-form piece featuring yourself in return, and we may be able to get a local salon to throw us a bone for hair."

"OK, OK," Maddy says. "Good start."

"Sorry," I ask. "I'm not really sure what all this means. Does that mean someone from those companies will help me sort of turn things around? Or will they give me free stuff?"

"Uhhhhmmm," Maddy looks at her team in the same manner she looked at Debbie during our lunch where they both were trying to communicate that they thought I was unhinged. "Well maybe, it will depend on what Arlo can negotiate. Typically, they will pay a fee for me to do a little promo shout out in the video or use their products or whatnot. Maybe they'll provide a discount code that I can plug so that my subscribers or followers can get a discount in an affiliate type sponsorship."

My face continues to fall even further. I naively thought my 23-year-old niece was going to single handedly revamp my life in a week. I'm now realizing that she is using me to get a paycheck while I air my dirty laundry to a bunch of strangers who will likely pick apart my appearance, lifestyle, and bad decisions. Maddy senses my sudden change in demeanor and quickly steps in.

"But I kinda like your makeover show idea," she scrambles. The team pick up their heads unclear of where Maddy is going with this. "What if we do go a bit retro with this concept. Hear me out team. I take a week or two to focus on getting a bunch of this content recorded and then we parcel it out. So we do a teaser introducing my dear aunt Jackie who is going through a tough time. She's let herself go in appearance, home, job blah blah." She turns to me, "sorry aunt Jack, just storyboarding here. Then a before and after of her apartment. Mainly a clean-up. Riff, maybe you can handle that bit. Jackie doesn't even need to be there. Then a quick bit about finding your passion and shots of Jackie using that recruiter site you mentioned, Arlo. Hair makeover, I can bring her to Darwin, and then maybe a Makeup Mecca outing."

Maddy gets up and is now scribbling on a large whiteboard in the corner of the room that has a big calendar and matrix on it. While she and her team mumble in hushed tones and use the word engagement as if it's a modifier that needs to precede every other word, I take a closer look at this giant whiteboard. Nearly every hour of Maddy's day is pre-ordained as prescribed content. The board lists where she will be having coffee, how she needs to showcase a sandwich or outfit, who she is hanging out with, and what points she has to highlight during every interaction. If the biggest offense a Gen Xer could think of at 23 was "selling out" the exact opposite is true for Maddy's generation. She and her team seem so afraid of not selling every moment that I wonder if they would know how to just spend an afternoon doing whatever they choose.

"What do you think aunt Jack?" Maddy asks in a tone similar to that used by her mother when she wants to me to think I'm being asked for input, but in reality she just wants me to be agreeable.

"I think I'm a little confused and overwhelmed Mads, if I'm being honest," I reply.

"How about you just leave everything to me," she says. "Riff, Arlo, and I will come to your apartment on..."

"Wednesday between 8 and 10," Janelle interjects.

"Wednesday, and we'll shoot some initial intro and

B-roll content. We'll meet you, see your place, just sort of baseline stuff. The team can get the lay of the land. And then we'll do a day, let's say the following week…" Maddy pauses.

"Thursday, I can block you out for the afternoon," Janelle says while typing information into a calendar.

"I'll meet you and we can curate a new look, hair, makeup, maybe do a quick shop," she looks to Riff and Arlo who discreetly nod their heads acknowledging that this plan was actionable. "And then, you know, when you get your job and finances all sorted, we can do an update and show how awesome it all turned out," she says encouragingly. "It'll be great."

The optimism that I arrived with, where I thought I'd have a new life by Friday was suddenly colliding with reality. I appreciate that a 23-year-old thinks that all you have to do is film a few clips, get a new haircut, and click apply to a job or two to get a lifetime of bad decisions back in check. I suddenly realize that this may not be the most productive form of "different" that I could've tried to shake my life up a bit.

"Well as long as all of this won't cost me anything," I joke, phrasing my statement as both a confirmation and a question, "I'm in."

"Yay!" Maddy exclaims. "Great, so we'll all come to your place Wednesday for that initial shoot for the baseline stuff, and then next Thursday we'll plan an afternoon revamp. In the meantime, get going on the job hunt and things will be fully turned around in no time." I responded with a fake smile to show that I was on board, but mostly unconvinced.

"We really gotta get going for the Coffee-con event, Mads," Janelle pipes up.

"Right. It was great seeing you aunt Jack and we'll see you later this week," she says dismissively while looking at her phone. "Janelle will text you when we're on our way over to your place. Feel free to take some nutrition bars on your way out. I did a sponsorship thing with them and the company sent me a ton of cases that I couldn't possibly eat through before they all expire. They are vegan, high protein, low carb, and locally sourced."

Maddy and her team turn to each other to start discussing something else and I suddenly get that same please-go-away-now feeling that I got during my layoff conference call. My inner Gen Xer turns this feeling of hurt into a defensive "whatever" and I get up and do as I'm told, shoveling about twenty nutrition bars into my bag before closing the door behind me.

Walking back to the L shaking my head, I have an entire conversation with myself about what just happened, what I agreed to, and what will happen next. To an outsider, I probably look much like Freddy does in the afternoons after he's spent the day drinking. An affable demeanor replaced by inappropriate outbursts, angry babbling, and misplaced facial expressions meant for someone the rest of the world can't see. Between inner monologue arguments I realize that my phone is ringing.

"Hey Liz," I answer. "So sorry I didn't call you back the other day, I got into a bit of a funk that is taking me a minute to get out of."

"Can you hear me?" she says in a whisper.

"Ya, is everything OK?" I respond, concerned.

"I'm at the office, so I can't talk loudly. But I wanted to call you to see if you've signed whatever papers the company sent you yet?" she asks.

"No," I reply. "Not yet. There was a mix-up with them and they actually sent them to Dan's. So I think I just threw them on the coffee table and haven't even taken a look at them."

"DON'T SIGN THEM!" she whisper-yells. "I just got out of a meeting with the higher ups. Their prior meeting was running late so I sorta sat in the back while they finished up. Apparently, a bunch of the other folks who were laid off have retained employment lawyers because they claim the company has been engaging in age discrimination practices. Everyone who got laid off was over 50 except for one person who was 43. I guess within the past two rounds of layoffs, the same demographics hold true and they are claiming a pattern of age discrimination."

"Whoa?" I interject.

"No kidding," she says. "I poked around a bit and found the name of the law firm they are all using. I'll text it to you. Reach out to them and see if you can add your name to the suit. It sounds like the company typically just settles these things to move on. But hopefully it will get you an infusion of cash until you can find something new."

"Liz, you are a true lifesaver," I acknowledge. "Thank you thank you!"

"You got it friend," she says. "Though please don't let anyone know you heard it from me. This place is getting mighty weird, but I need to keep this job as long as I can."

"My lips are sealed!"

"OK, texting now and talk to you soon. Good luck!"

Within moments she texts me the contact information of the law firm the rest of the laid off employees are using. I ride the L home, walk in the apartment, dump my bounty of free nutrition bars in a bowl on the kitchen counter and begin the search around my apartment for the work separation papers. I'd been so mad at Dan when I retrieved them that morning, that I can't exactly remember where in the chaos heap of my clutter that I threw them when I'd walked in the door.

An hour later I find the envelope under a pile of junk mail and dirty laundry. I proceed to e-mail the lawyer and within minutes receive a call from her assistant to get my information and the scoop. The case of the other laid off employees is already taking shape and she informs me that they would gladly represent me as well to add fuel to the fire. My mind races a bit as the thought of paying lawyer fees makes my stomach turn as I am still on a payment plan with my divorce lawyer. However, she assuages my anxiety and tells me that any fee would be taken out of a settlement or even be considered part of the settlement that my previous employer would have to pay.

She tells me that the next step is for me to scan copies of my documents and send them along to the firm and they would handle the rest. Given that "set it and forget it" has always been my work mantra, it seems fitting that this may be the way forward as well. The assistant warns me that it can sometimes take large companies a while to settle, as they like to make former employees who engage counsel worry in an effort to make folks settle for less. However, she encourages me to hang tight and trust them. As someone with minimal savings who would soon need to start using her credit card as a bank account, this wasn't exactly music to my ears.

I hang up with the firm, scan the papers, snack on an overpriced but free-to-me granola bar and decide to finally buckle down and attempt to create a resume out of thin air. I go down a resume 101 rabbit hole that entails reading about modern philosophies and strategies for job seeking. The last time I created a resume, I remember padding the truth in order to hide my lack of experience and years in the workforce. Apparently at this point in my life, the key is to hide my years of experience to avoid age discrimination and being deemed overqualified for available positions. The thought of this literally makes me laugh out loud.

One search result did catch my eye. It was an ad for an AI program to help craft and format a modern, optimized, resume promising minimal effort on the part of the end user. While this ordinarily would've received an eye roll and raised the red flag of my over sensitive internal bullshit detector, I figure if AI appears to be taking my job, the least it could do is help me find my next one.

When prompted with questions, I enter a bunch of information that will either inspire my new career identity or inspire a nefarious hacker to steal my actual identity. I tell myself that the risk is worth it, given that if someone wants the keys to my rubble of a castle, best of luck to them. Either way after about a half an hour I download a document that makes me sound competent, employable, and hopefully younger than I actually am.

The bigger challenge is to figure out where to send said resume and what I actually want to do next. I'd fallen into the editorial field after college following several years of working odd jobs including front desk assistant at a copy shop, development roles at non-profits, and a sales assistant at an art gallery. I looked at descriptions for jobs that had titles akin to my latest one at Reed and felt like Goldilocks looking for a place to lay her head. Some jobs were entry level with titles that made them sound like they were heads of state. Others described roles responsible for managing entire divisions but touting salaries of less than half of what I'd been making. None of the jobs I was reviewing really felt like the perfect combination of what I'd want to do and what I'd be good at. Had I just aged out of the job market completely? Or was I never in the right career field to begin with?

Recognizing that beggars can't be choosers I set out to apply to anything that seems like I would be remotely qualified. After an hour of key word searches, AI matching, and a few online personality tests, this amounts to applying for a whopping two jobs. While not exactly a heroic achievement, I consider it a win.

That evening, satisfied that my life might be moving in a direction other than downward, I pop a weed gummy in my mouth and decide to dip my toe into another type of online search. I download a dating app.

Slightly high, mildly insecure, and vaguely

optimistic, I upload several photos that Maddy took of me within the past year. The app instructs me to answer a few questions that showcase my personality and what I am looking for. To be fair, I have no idea if I have thoughts on either of those topics, but I make an effort. I try to come off as fun and flirty, without the need to worry about overpromising and underdelivering if I had to meet someone in person.

> **Describe a perfect Sunday date**: Sleeping in, taking a walk with a fancy coffee, and swapping that coffee for an afternoon cocktail garnished with conversation.
>
> **If money and qualifications were no object, what job would you like?** I would enjoy the security of being highly educated and independently wealthy.
>
> **Describe yourself in 5 words:** Urban, redhead, skeptical, optimist, Gen X

While I'm not sure my answers in combination with the pictures will garner a lot of "engagement," as Maddy and her team would say, I honestly can't be bothered with investing any more time or energy in my profile. Instead, I'm more interested in diving into the slow shuffle and swipe of my potential mating options.

The idea that I have a seemingly endless supply of dating partners to put in a virtual shopping cart is both exhilarating and overwhelming. Unlike the sad collection of jobs at my disposal, at first glance, the number of men at my disposal seems plentiful. I'd met Dan the old-fashioned way, by drunkenly making out with him in a dark corner of a dive bar after cozying up at the jukebox halfway through his selection of five dollars-worth of songs. The progression of the Velvet Underground, into the Magnetic Fields into Portishead, made me need to know this man who would have the audacity to subject a room full of strangers to a moody mix of alternative brooding tunes. I know how to judge a person by their musical tastes, but the concept of virtually judging people based on a few photos and three sentences, which I suspect most people have AI answer, is foreign to me. I take it as an opportunity to dip my toe into the dating pool without drowning off the bat.

I begin liking a few profiles based on some kind eyes, a funny quip, or an interesting photo background and within 15 minutes receive several message alerts. While I recognize that the app won't inspire an epistolary exchange on the level of Jane Austen, I'm a bit perplexed by the first messages I receive. One simply says "Sup?" Another is just two eggplant and peach emojis. A third catches me off guard as it's two dick pics. The dick pics were of one White penis and one Black penis with a note that says, "so hard for you." The person couldn't even bother to use two stolen photos representing the same race or ethnicity, let alone the same man. I am utterly dumbfounded. Much like my initial meeting with Maddy and her team, I've never experienced the rise and fall of hope so drastically in such a short period of time.

Dick pics burned into my brain and my weed gummy kicking in in full force, I plug my phone in, stick an old Mazzy Star album on the turntable, and go to bed hopeful that the next day will be better than the last.

FOUR

I wake up to banging at my door. I look at my phone and see it's 8:15 in the morning. I also see that I have about 15 unread dating app messages that look to be more versions of three letter intros and phallic fruit and vegetable DMs. The banging continues, so I pop up braless, pantsless, and dry mouthed and open the door worried that my building is on fire.

"Everyone, I'd like you to meet Jackie," Maddy says brightly, dressed flawlessly and made up impeccably. Arlo is standing next to her filming with his phone. "Jackie is my favorite aunt who is going through a rough time right now. She lost her job, her husband, and her sense of style and self. The MadLove squad and I are going to help her sprinkle some sparkle back in her world."

"Madeline," I scowl. "What the hell time is it?"

"We're doing a *live* stream Jackie," she says giving me a side-eye. "Just showing my fab followers what we're starting with and hopefully showing them that all it takes is a little MadLove in their lives to turn things around. Arlo will follow me as I give everyone a tour."

Maddy steps away from me and continues inside my apartment, talking non-stop as if she owns the place.

"I was skeptical about this whole idea," Riff whispers to me, "but you really roughed things up to help emphasize a dramatic before. Thanks for doing that. I think that'll translate to some major makeover content and really boost engagement."

"Riff, I like that you think that I'm some sort of marketing genius like Maddy, but this is just me waking up to people running through my place unannounced. A little notice would've been nice!" I reply in a very loud whisper.

"Janelle told you Wednesday from 8-10 when you were at the loft," they snap back. "Wait, so this is how you really live? I thought you were laying it on thick for the cameras."

When I don't respond they give me a sad up and down look, touch my arm and then walk into the bedroom area of my studio to join Maddy and Arlo. I follow soon after trying to remember if in the chaos of my messy bed they would find a half empty bottle of weed gummies and a vibrator lying on top of the covers.

"So, everyone stay tuned in the coming weeks to

see how MadLove transforms my aunt Jackie's life," Maddy pouts with a slight duck lip pose to the camera. "Sending MadLove to you all." She winks, mock air kisses, and flashes a peace sign.

Arlo points at her signaling they have stopped livestreaming. Her demeanor and voice change and she's instantly back to being the Maddy I know.

"That was perfect, Jack," she smiles. "Thanks for making everything such a mess so we really look like we have a lot to work with." Arlo and Riff have already moved on and are using tape measures and laser pointers as they walk around my apartment.

"Maddy," I say sternly though still half asleep, "your grandmother follows you on social media. As does uncle Dan…"

"Along with several hundred thousand other people," she says proudly.

"I really appreciate you helping me out, hon, I really do," I concede. "But I don't want you putting it out there that I'm like a sad sack living in a gutter or something. This stuff lives on forever."

"Oh, don't worry aunt Jackie," she brushes me off and resumes texting. "Everyone knows that content is a bit exaggerated and curated."

"Do they?" I ask.

"Are you allowed to do any minor construction?" Riff yells from the bathroom.

"No," I respond with concern. They come back into the main living area looking disappointed.

"I love all those 90s vintage t-shirts you have on the floor of your closet," Arlo comments. "Do you run a vintage shop or something?"

"No," I laugh. "Those are just my shirts that I bought back in the day that I still I wear." They all give each other knowing and judgmental glances. I'm immediately confused as to why my shirts which were cool two seconds ago when they thought that I was selling them to others, have become pathetic when they realize that they're in my closet because I haven't updated my wardrobe in decades.

"You could probably sell those," Arlo adds. "You know, if you need the cash. The 90s are hot right now and everyone is buying vintage."

I almost launch into a righteous speech about how they should refrain calling something vintage unless it is from the 1940s or 50s. But thankfully I stop myself when I do the math and realize that to these kids the 1990s are the equivalent to the 1950s for me.

"Maybe when we get her some new clothes, she can sell some of the old ones," Maddy hints.

"Already getting some traction on the live stream," Riff interrupts looking at his phone. "Not major, but a lot of interest and sympathy for Jackie. Lots of people have older moms like her and can relate."

They continue scrolling reading out random comments. "Someone else says that we should get her a good bra fitting. That's actually a good idea, I wonder if we can partner with…"

The team continues to talk about me, my home, and now even my boobs in front of me as if they're figuring out ways to market vile tasting green juice to unsuspecting carnivores. I stand there making faces and hand gestures that no one seems to notice or care about.

"OK," Maddy looks up, squinting at me, plotting her next move. "So next week aunt Jack you will come meet me at the loft. Me, you, and Janelle will go out and do a little shopping, we'll do some makeup, deal with your hair, that kind of thing. While we're doing that, Arlo, Riff and maybe a couple of interns will come over here and give the place the MadLove treatment. Then we'll do a big reveal and then parse the content out over the weeks that follow and see how we do."

"Do you have a spare key you can give us?" Riff asks. Suddenly self-conscious, I tuck my forearm under my breasts and over my t-shirt and walk over to look through the top kitchen junk drawer. I hand over a key.

"How are you making out on the job and love life front?" Maddy asks. I look at her incredulously. Does she really think I've found a new job and love of my life in a matter of days?

"I applied to a few things and joined a dating app," I say. "Basically, I'm just getting a bunch of dick pics and fruit emojis from morons. On the dating apps, that is. I haven't even gotten so much as a dick pic from the job stuff."

"Well, you may need to lower your expectations on the job stuff, aunt Jack," she says nonchalantly clearly not acknowledging my joke. "You had a remote lazy girl job for all those years. I think those are getting harder to come by particularly for Boomers."

"GEN-X!" I correct defensively while rolling my eyes. "Seriously, why can no one remember that we exist? And I'm not a lazy person…"

"No, it's just a term," she responds. "Like jobs where you don't have to try too hard and sorta just get paid. I mean they're great for some people, but like after a while you realize you sorta lose your edge, don't keep up on skills, and then when someone up high in the big corporate office looks closely at who they really need, they cut you and you're sorta…"

"Fucked," I sigh.

"Exactly," she says. While I resent the term itself implying that I'm a lazy person, based on that definition I'm pretty sure that's exactly what my job always was or had at least become over the last few years. My complacency of thinking I was living the dream has suddenly turned into my living nightmare.

"Janelle is texting," Riff announces. "We should get going to get you changed for the next shoot."

"Wait," I interject. "So when you guys are in my apartment doing your whole MadLove thing when I'm not here, are you just doing to be, ya know, moving furniture around for Feng shui and stuff? You won't be throwing anything out, or really touching my stuff, right?"

"Riff and Arlo won't throw anything out," Maddy confirms instinctively. Though both people look disappointed by her comment. "Though they may go through all those boxes over there and try to put things in their place so it doesn't look like you live in a storage unit."

"Fair enough," I agree.

"Great," she kisses me on the cheek. "See you next week and keep going on the job thing." As she steps toward the door, I'm taken aback that both Arlo and Riff hug me goodbye. Previously, they both seemed to react to me and my surroundings like dirty laundry. Am I misjudging them? Or do I somehow rate higher now that I will be the subject of their content?

I lock the door and crawl back into bed. Scrolling through my phone I dismiss the pointless dating app notifications and messages, seemingly having attracted nothing but bots and those running phishing scams. I click on a LinkedIn notification from a recruiter wanting to connect after seeing my "Open to Work" banner. When I'd mentioned to Maddy that updating that banner was one of my job-hunting tactics, she recoiled and told me that that was perceived as being a bit desperate and "thirsty." Once again, I reminded her that I was both of those things on pretty much any type of app she could think of and I was OK with owning my status. The recruiter's message includes a link to a calendar to book an introductory call and I schedule it for early the following week in hopes that something more exciting comes my way in the meantime.

After some additional doom scrolling, including a peek at my declining bank balance and increasing credit card balance, I fully embrace denial, get dressed, and head out for some coffee. I exit my building and start to turn right.

"Jack-ay?!" a man's voice calls out. I look around for Freddy, but don't see him. "Over here in the van." Brian the plumber is parked out front sitting in a van emblazoned with the Windy City Waterworks logo on the side.

"Oh hey," I smile and walk over. "Is this some sort of remote plumbing job where you do it from the van?" I joke.

"Feels like it," he replies. "This is the second time I've been out here for a scheduled appointment with your downstairs neighbor, and she's a no show."

"Can the management company let you in?" I ask.

"Since it's a non-emergency thing they don't like to let you into people's places," he says. "So I'm gonna give her like 30 minutes and hopefully she'll remember." He pauses to check his phone and then looks up. "So, how've you been?"

"Pretty good, actually," I say. "I think the little pep-talk you gave me the last time you were here actually inspired me to try some new things. Whether or not they pan out is a different story. My niece who is a big social media star is trying to make my shitty life into content for her channel which she thinks may help, so I'm even giving that a whirl." I feel myself using self-deprecation to make my situation sound more "funny/quirky" and less "actually desperate."

"Don't be so hard on yourself. You are alive, you are a pretty woman, your life could be way shittier, trust me," he winks. "I've seen thousands of apartments, houses, basements, and all sorts of stuff around this city. You don't have it so bad."

"Fair point," I concede. "I'm heading over to grab a coffee, did you want anything? Or, I mean, if you want to you can join me unless you have to wait out front." Did I just ask him to coffee? Why do I feel like I'm in 9th grade all of sudden?

"Uhhh..." he looks down at the clock on his phone.

"No pressure," I add quickly. I worry that I've overstepped some boundary of the plumber-client relationship. Either that or perhaps the state of me is way worse than I anticipated if a giant man wearing overalls would prefer to sit in a van rather than be seen having a cup of coffee with me.

"No, it's not that," he laughs. "I just gotta be careful about travelling too far because work tracks my phone. It's both a Big Brother and a safety thing. We had some bad apples join the company last year. They were doing things like squeezing in off-the-books jobs with the company's supplies and equipment and pocketing the cash. They would claim their morning appointments just got more complicated than they anticipated and just rush through those jobs to pick up side work. And then on the safety side, we did have a guy get carjacked at gunpoint for the tools and stuff. So, they said they are tracking us to help, but ya never know."

"Ahhh," I say, feeling relieved his initial trepidation was not related to me at all. "Well, I'm just going to Wormhole, down the block. Your little tracker dot would barely move." I grin and hope I'm not seeming too desperate or trying too hard to talk him out of his polite excuse.

"That, I can do," he smiles. He rolls up the window and gets out of the van. At 5'10" I rarely feel dwarfed when standing next to anyone, but he is a good six inches taller than me. Sporting worker overalls and large boots, with graying reddish-brown hair and a big mustache, he looks a bit like Paul Bunyan if he happened to grow up in Chicago. We walk down the block and head into the 1980s themed coffee shop.

"Hey Jackie," Miles says. He's the thirtysomething barista who's been trying to break into sketch comedy for as long as I've been coming to this shop. "The usual?"

"Yeah, thanks Miles. And you can get my friend here whatever he wants too," I add.

"Sorry, buddy," Brian smiles as he scans the extensive menu hanging above the counter. "I'm not used to all these options. I'm more of a how-long-has-this-coffee-in-this-pot-been-sitting-here kinda guy. So, I'm a little overwhelmed."

"Are you adventurous?" I ask.

"I'll try anything once," he laughs.

"Give him a rosemary cardamom latte," I instruct.

"Wow," Brian says. "OK, let's give that a go." I grab my wallet out of my jacket pocket and with his big tree trunk of an arm Brian waves me off and gives me a wink as he slaps down his credit card on the card reader. I see he leaves Miles a very generous tip and I respond with a gesture of thanks. "It's the least I can do, you're opening my eyes to flavor profiles my blue-collar taste buds would never have encountered." We both laugh.

We grab a table against the wall and await our coffees. The café has art, movie memorabilia and objects from the 80s strewn about and Brian points and comments on much of it telling me about the lunchbox he's pretty sure he had. He has a booming voice that one wouldn't necessarily consider "inside voice," that I gather both corresponds to his size and years of being around machines and tools that clang and bang. When our coffees are up, he grabs them and returns to the table suggesting that there's no rush to get him back to his van.

"Were you a big 80s fan?" he asks. "You know the music and style and stuff?"

"Of course," I agree. "I had the big hair, the shoulder pads, and was always down at the record store buying the latest and greatest. Though I think I was always a bit angsty and really came into my own in the 90s. Sometimes I feel like my angry or 'whatever' phase never left me, for better or worse. I mean I still quote 90s movies like *Reality Bites* and *Singles* to my sister on a weekly basis."

"I've never seen those." He takes a long sip of coffee and his eyes light up. "This is amazing by the way."

"Wait. What? Really? You never saw the quintessential movies of our generation?" I exaggerate.

"I was off jumping into marriage and parenthood

way too early in the 90s that I think I missed everything that we were supposed to do," he says with an edge of regret.

"Maybe you're better off," I reply. "I still have this mindset that it sucks to 'sell out' or whatnot that was ingrained in me from back then. Meanwhile my 23-year-old niece is basically a millionaire simply for broadcasting to the world every moment and meal of her day. I dunno…"

"You gotta run your own race, Jackie," Brian proclaims. "At the end of the day you can only make yourself happy, it doesn't matter what anyone else thinks. I started my own plumbing company when I was 31, kinda got caught up in thinking I needed to be a boss to make it and really 'show everyone' that I was worthy of, I honestly don't know what."

"Wow," I reacted.

"Well fact is, being a boss and business owner sucks," he laughs. "And then your ex-wife takes half of the profits in a divorce and I was left thinking, is this what I really want to be doing with my time on the planet? Like I like the plumbing stuff and talking to and helping people. But I don't want to have conversations about health insurance, business insurance, is this guy showing up to work, do I need to deal with a customer complaint for a job I didn't even do, equipment buying, hiring, firing, all of it. I didn't go to business school, I went to school to be a plumber and that's what I want to do."

"But having seen it from both sides, does it really get under your skin when you find out things like they're tracking you on your phone?" I ask. "Or, if your company is anything like mine was, someone half your age is now your boss even though they've never actually done half the things you've done?"

"Oh, that definitely gets under my skin," he says. "But, ya know, if they want to take on all that other crap that I honestly don't want to do, so be it. I can rest assured that I get my steady paycheck, insurance, and can maybe one day retire. They're my coworkers, and while a lot of the guys are good friends, if anyone rubs me the wrong way, after quitting time I don't have to see them."

"I think that's a good attitude. My job's been remote for so many years that I think there were times when I forgot that they weren't with me all the time because I was still having arguments with them in my head hours after I closed my computer."

"I don't know where your parents ended up," he acknowledges. "But mine ended up in a retirement community in Arizona. Whenever I go visit them, I look around and see a bunch of old raisiny looking people out there baking in the desert. They all drive similar white cars, live in similar beige houses, and are all getting and talking about similar diseases. It doesn't matter if they were CEOs or janitors during their earlier years, everyone ends up in the same boat. So, you might as well enjoy the boat ride along the way, ya know."

"What did your parents do before they retired?" I ask.

"My dad owned a bar up in Jefferson Park," he said. "My youngest brother bought it from him and still runs it. I'm there most Friday and Saturday nights, sometimes helping out, sometimes just at the end of the bar giving my brother a hard time and shooting the shit with the regulars. It's O'Brien's."

"Wait, wait, wait, wait," I interrupt waving my hands. "Hold up. Does that mean your name is Brian O'…"

"Brien," he completes the sentence running his hands through his hair and mustache, smiling sheepishly. "Yes indeed. First one is with an A, the second one is with an E."

My mouth drops.

"That right there ends any anger issues you may have had with your parents, right?" he laughs. "I'm actually Brian O'Brien the third. My mom apparently fought to have the legacy stop with my dad, but clearly Dad won. Middle brother is Dave, he works in tech or sales or something that I'm not quite sure about. He's the smarty. And then Chris is the youngest and owns and runs the bar."

"Wow," I smile.

"You?" he asks. "What's your family like?"

"My mom still lives up in my childhood home in Rogers Park," I explain. "She's a...*tough* woman, I guess I would say." I pause for a minute and am enamored by how much eye contact he's giving me. It's focused, in a non-creepy way, that just makes me feel like he's really engaged and wants to hear more. Straddling the line of trying not to overshare and bore him to pieces, but give him some context, I continue. "We always butted heads and still do to some degree. She's sort of, all about her, which has gotten worse as she's gotten older. I'm not sure if it's the start of dementia, some long-undiagnosed mental condition, or maybe just her personality. Whatever it is, I try to keep a friendly distance. My dad died of cancer about 10 years ago. My sister Debbie, who I'm super close with, and her husband Tom live up in Evanston. Debbie has two kids, Maddy and Cameron so I'm the fun aunt to them. Though like I mentioned Maddy is turning out to be more of an adult than I am these days."

"That sounds like a small and close-knit group though," he says kindly. "I think growing up in the bar with brothers, cousins, and all that chaos there was always a part of me that was like, wouldn't it be nice to just go home and have it be quiet?" he laughs.

His phone buzzes on the table and he picks it up and looks at it.

"Your neighbor just called the main office and told them she needs to reschedule," he rolls his eyes. "Would be great if she'd done that *before* I'd come out here. Hey, but at least I got a really good cup of coffee, some movie recommendations, and excellent conversation."

"Likewise," I say as we start to stand up.

"Thanks for the coffee, guy," he says boomingly as he waves to Miles the barista. "Really good." Miles gives him a chin nod as he continues helping another customer.

We begin walking back to his truck and I start to feel a bit sad that this interaction has to end. It's the first time in a long time that anyone, man, woman, or child has talked to me just to learn about me and not because they want something or want me to do something.

"Jack-AYYYYY!" a voice yells from behind. Brian and I both spin around to see Freddy jogging a few steps to catch up with us. "Looks like you snagged yourself a lumberjack. Did ya take a ride on his log?" he starts cackling uncontrollably.

"Freddy," I say with gritted teeth and an annoyed glare.

"I'm Brian," Brian extends his hand to him.

"Hey, hey, my man," Freddy over exaggeratedly

shakes his hand. "No disrespect Jack-ayyy. Calm down girl. You need to get some wood in your life, you're too uptight." He cackles again.

"Freddy likes to announce my arrival and ask for monetary grants to buy booze," I say sarcastically.

"She ain't wrong," Freddy confesses.

"Well let me contribute to the cause," Brian smiles. He pulls out a 20-dollar bill from his pocket and hands it to Freddy.

"Oh, Brian," I start.

"I like this lumberjack mofo more than I like you Jack-ayyy," Freddy smiles. "You're welcome back any time, my man." Freddy gives him a fist bump and takes off across the street and I look up at Brian in a why-did-you-do-that sort of way.

"I've been dealing with guys like Freddy my whole life," Brian says. "In my experience, it's best to just help them out and get on their good side and hope one day they use the money for coffee rather than booze."

"Fair point," I reluctantly agree. "But he tends to get worse as the day goes on. Though maybe that means he'll not pester me for a few days."

We get to Brian's van and I'm not exactly sure how to part ways. Thankfully he takes the lead.

"I'm a hugger, so brace yourself," he laughs. He delivers the biggest and most comforting bear hug that I've had in years and part of me doesn't want to let go. "Don't worry, the overalls are still clean. This was my first call of the day. I'll probably be back here next week, assuming your neighbor doesn't blow me off again. So hopefully I'll see you again then and I can reconnect the dishwasher in your place."

"Sounds great," I smile, realizing this man I just talked to like he was a free therapist just suddenly snapped back into the role of building plumber.

His phone starts ringing and he answers it and begins talking to his office manager as he waves and gets in the driver's seat. I go inside replaying the conversation in my head and feeling more like an embodied person living in the world than I have in years.

FIVE

While work was clearly never my priority or passion, it gave me a reason to wake up every day. Without a job, nor disposable income to fritter away the day, I'm surprised at how challenging it can be to fill my days, particularly over a weekend.

By Sunday late morning I'd semi-cleaned my apartment, Facetimed with Debbie three times, applied to many random jobs that seemed like I would be a shoe-in for, painted my nails, and tried and applied nearly all of the skin cleaning, moisturizing, and wrinkle-reducing free samples I'd collected over the years. I'd also listened to a dozen podcasts, baked a batch of cookies, gone through my college yearbook and Googled everyone that I vaguely remembered but lost track of, tried on half my closet until I got depressed, and had random banter with the few men on the dating app that hadn't opened with a picture or emoji of genitals. It's as if I took all the activities that occupied my time during the pandemic and squished them into a weekend.

By lunchtime on Sunday, I decide I need to do one thing I'd been putting off since my layoff. I take a deep breath, grab a plate of cookies to have them nearby, and hit my mother's number in my phone contacts. After three rings, a sense of relief washes over me as I assume she's not going to pick up and I can just leave a message thereby getting credit for the phone call without having to go through whatever emotional abuse she has in store for me. By ring four, that fantasy was thwarted.

"Well, it's about time," she answers.

"And hello to you too, mother," I respond.

"I was wondering when you'd call," she says. "I saw you looking like a hot mess on Maddy's MadLove TV show and I was appalled. Jacqueline, the world could see you weren't wearing a bra or pants. I raised you better than that. Don't you have any dignity?"

"It's not television, ma," I correct. "It's Maddy's social media."

"I don't care what you call it," she doubles down. "Social media is television for people nowadays. Even more people see that than some television programs. How do you expect to get another husband if you are showing the world that you live like a slob and look like a mess?"

While this is in some respects what I was afraid of when calling my mother, I'm pleasantly surprised that her focus seems to solely be on what I was wearing and the condition of my apartment. What she didn't seem to pick up on from my video appearance was the fact that I was now laid off and heading into a very uncertain financial situation. If she wants to concentrate her worry and criticisms on my poor outfit choices impacting my ability to attract a new mate, so be it.

"We were playing it up for the camera, ma," I suggest. I put her on speakerphone so I can check out of this disaster of a conversation and sort through another unopened box from my move. "Maddy came over super early and unexpectedly so that she could get some good footage of me and my place looking at its worst. She's going to do a makeover on me. Remember how Oprah used to do those on her shows? Well it will be like that. So she wanted to make sure everyone thought I looked really horrible before so that the after looks that much better."

"Well, that may be the case," she calms down. "But you know when things go on the Internet they are there forever. So now anyone who Googles you can find out what a slob you are. And for God-sakes, Jacqueline, wear a bra and dye your hair. You look older than I do now. I mean I know I look super young for my age, all my friends tell me that and even the young man at the Starbucks tried to hit on me the other day, but you just look haggard."

"Ok, mom," I sigh and roll my eyes while shoving a cookie into my mouth. I wonder why I had to inherit my mother's shapeless butt rather than her over-developed self-esteem and sense of confidence. "Understood. I'll make sure it doesn't happen again. So how are you?"

I'd intended to tell her about the layoff and immediately assuage any concerns she voiced by putting on an air that I had it all under control. However, since she came into the call so hot, I decide to abort that plan. While talking and dealing with my mother can be a challenge, the one good thing about her is that her extreme self-centeredness makes the conversation easy to redirect. So by simply asking her how she is, I'm able to buy myself a good 15 to 20 minutes of not having to talk about myself.

"Well, I was good until those new neighbors moved in," she says. "Did I tell you about them? The ones with the four little kids? They have the nerve to put in one of those big trampolines in their backyard. Now we have that high fence in the back. The one that daddy put in when you girls were little. When those kids jump on that trampoline, they tower over the fence by like four feet. It's like their parents don't even care if they fly off and break their arms or are out there disturbing me when I'm trying to read on the patio. You know parents these days are not the same as when we raised you. They just have no thought for other people."

My mother continues with her monologue for a solid ten minutes. At one point I put the phone on mute, put it on the coffee table, go to the bathroom, refill my glass of water, and return without her so much as noticing I'd been gone. She is a social woman, with many friends in her neighborhood, which always perplexes me. Both that others would want to be friends with her, given they rarely have the opportunity to get a word in edgewise, and that she still has so much conversation left over to tell everyone else.

Just as I was wondering if she would notice if I took an afternoon nap while on with her, I hear her call me by name.

"I mean really, can you believe that Jackie? Jackie?" she asks. I take her off of mute.

"No mom, I can't," I have no idea what I've just agreed with.

"So, when is this makeover show happening with Maddy?" she asks.

"I'm not sure. I think she's filming some stuff for it next week and then will have to edit and all that," I say.

"Well, you be nice to her," she warns. "That little girl is such a hard worker. Can you believe she owns such a big expensive apartment at 23? I mean Debbie knew what she was doing when she raised her. You're 52 and can't even bother to make your own bed in the shoebox of an apartment that you have to RENT."

"Mom," I interrupt. "I actually have to go. I'm meeting someone for lunch shortly."

"Is it a man?" she asks. "Is it a date? Are you dating anyone."

"Love you mom," I don't provide an answer.

"Well come see me soon, honey," she says sweetly. "You never know how long I have left."

She hangs up and I am left with feelings of both irritation and melancholy. I want to just be outright angry at her, but then she makes closing remarks hinting at her own demise and I feel pangs of guilt and regret despite her inability to be anything but condescending. I know I should address these feelings with some sort of meditation, feelings of gratitude, or some other coping mechanism, but instead pick up my phone and open the dating app. If my mother can't show me love and affection, maybe Javier312 can.

Javier is one of the dating app people with whom I actually exchanged a few coherent sentences over the last few days. Looks-wise, from his photos, he appears to be a slightly older, Latino version of Dan. Thick black rim glasses, he's wearing a beanie in every photo, and he seems obsessed with barbequing as three of his four photos seem to involve the act of eating something grilled or grilling something to eat. Twenty years ago, simply being able to exchange a few sentences that didn't refer to genitals and showing off one's grilling skills wouldn't have gotten a second look from me. But it seems times have changed and apparently Javier312 is the top of the dating crop for me.

"Up for grabbing a drink later today?" I write through the app.

"Sure," he responds before I even have time to put my phone back down on the coffee table.

This riveting level of conversation continues with a few more exchanges until we confirm to meet at a dive bar in Logan Square for a happy hour cocktail. The bar is far enough away from my regular neighborhood haunts that if the meetup turns out to be a disaster no one I know will be a witness and I can easily avoid ever going to the place again.

I stare at my closet and realize that I may literally have nothing to wear. I have a few work-appropriate outfits for when I would have to go into the office for annual meetings and trainings, and then the rest of my clothes are 1990s band t-shirts, black leggings, and a few pairs of jeans that would qualify as "sorta fitting." I have one t-shirt dress that, at this point, is beginning to look simply like a long old t-shirt. The only other thing hanging up is a brightly colored bathing suit coverup dress that I borrowed from Debbie three years ago that I wore to a *Three's Company* themed party because I thought it made me look like Mrs. Roper.

I look at my watch and realize I need to get a move on if I'll be remotely on time. I stare for a few more minutes before determining that Mrs. Roper will be going out for a drink. I throw on some minimal makeup, put some product in my hair so that my red half-curls-half-frizz don't make me look like I'm actually trying to be Mrs. Roper and I throw a condom in my purse for good luck. I'd bought a box right after I found out about Dan's affair in hopes that I could go out and have steamy revenge sex with random strangers as retaliation. Instead, the box has sat unopened in my nightstand and at this point is probably nearing its expiration date.

Twenty minutes later I'm sitting at the end of the bar, halfway through a martini, more nervous than I've been in years. Trying not to gulp my drink down, and failing miserably, I look up when the door opens and see the man that I think is my date. He's backlit by the light from the door entering the dark bar so I'm wary about acknowledging him until he approaches first.

"Jackie?" he asks. He's wearing the exact outfit he wore in one of his pictures, but he must've used a filter or something on the photo because in person he looks a bit older, rounder, and far from

Latino. He's also a good three inches shorter than he mentioned which makes me wonder if I'll tower over him when I stand up.

"Hey!" I smile. "Javier, I take it?" He smiles as he pulls a stool up next to me.

"I go by Javier312 on the app, but it's actually Johnny," he reveals. I cock my head slightly confused. "I feel like the name helps me cast a wider net of replies, if you know what I mean."

"Oh," I say, though still a bit confused as to what he did indeed mean.

"You're very bright and festive," he says. "I like a woman who's spicy."

"I don't know about spicy," I laugh.

"Well maybe I can taste you later and find out," he says with a facial expression akin to a cartoon character about to eat a meal. Taken aback I flinch a bit at the comment. "Just kiddin' with you." He laughs and touches my arm. My feelings of nerves start to merge with a fight or flight instinct that I try to suppress. He orders a drink and signals to the bartender to bring me another martini, which I'm both happy and a little skeptical about.

"So have you lived in the neighborhood long?" I ask trying to make the conversation a bit more mundane.

"About 15 years," he says, "You'll see my house later and you'll look perfect in it. I love color, particularly in my bedroom."

I stare back at him confused. I assumed all the over-sexualized banter and bravado I was receiving on the dating app was akin to trolling from the safety of one's couch. I didn't expect to be getting any of it in real life. When I was young, if I'd gotten a similar icky feeling from someone, I might've instinctively said something off-putting to extricate myself and walk away never giving the guy another thought. In my current vulnerable state, feeling lucky to have secured a date at all, I feel compelled to stick around and see if perhaps I can break through this guy's prickly exterior to reveal a relatable person lurking underneath.

"Let's not get ahead of ourselves, Johnny," I laugh trying to brush his comment off. When the bartender puts down my second martini, I ask him for a water as well.

"Water?" Johnny asks. "We're just getting started and ready to party, don't start on water yet."

"So, what is it that you do for work? I realize I never asked?" I try to change the topic again. Johnny seemed to be a bit like some sort of Bobblehead doll you'd pick up at Spencer Gifts in the mall in the 1980s, where if you pushed a button, innuendo came out in a pre-recorded voice.

"Oh, I see how it's gonna be. It's gonna be like one of those job interview dates. Ok, I feel you," he says. He moves in closer and swivels his barstool so that he's facing me and my legs are now between his. His voice drops down to a low almost whisper. "I do a lot of things, but what I really want is to do them to you."

Caught off guard, I literally laugh in his face. I assume he's trying out some sort of improv character known as Come-On Man. He stares back at me with the same intensity he's been showing the whole time we've been talking. I then realize that he's not pretending to be some sort of pick-up line touting sex-bot, but that he truly may think this is the way to attract women.

"Wait, I'm sorry," I say. "Are you being serious right now?"

"You have a sexy laugh," he smirks.

"Javier, I mean, Johnny" I say skeptically. "You're cute and seem like a nice guy, but I came out to get to know you. You know the real you, have a conversation. That kind of thing? I think you can drop the act and just, be the real you."

"I think you're cute too, baby," he replies. He brings his knees together slightly, trapping my legs between his. "And I'm happy to show you the real me." He puts his hands on my face and before I have time to react his tongue is plunging into my mouth with the intrusiveness of a dentist's gloved finger probing for gum disease. I free my arm and push on his shoulder while my head lurches back.

"Dude!" I yell. "What the fuck?"

I startle him and he releases the grip with his knees. I sit there stunned as the bartender looks up from his phone at the other end of the bar, hoping that he doesn't need to get involved.

"Damn," Johnny says while putting up his hands. "I didn't know you were one of those cold bitches." His voice has gotten louder than his sex-bot voice, as if he's trying to ensure that those in the bar who may be watching realize the problem is me, not him.

"OK," I say while throwing twenty bucks on the bar, gathering my bag, and standing up. "I think we're done here."

"Cunt," he says flatly and under his breath. I glare back at him. "I'm not into chubby, old, ginger, prudes anyway. I was just trying to throw an old bitch a bone, as community service, that'll teach me...."

"Are you serious, right now, asshole?" I say loudly.

"Uh oh," he starts talking to the bar in general. "We got ourselves a Karen about to ask for the manager."

I roll my eyes, knowing that once the Karen moniker has been publicly thrown out, anything I say will be taken out of context, recorded, or otherwise misconstrued rendering me unable to stand up for myself against this man's unwanted advances. There's nothing I can do other than wave at the bartender as I leave, hope that this man doesn't do this to another woman, and delete the dating app account the moment I get home.

I do just that when I get home. I also text Debbie and arrange to go to her house for lunch tomorrow for a hug and a pep talk. I sit on the couch replaying the whole incident in my head. I get mad at myself for actually spending several minutes trying to think if I did anything wrong to make that situation happen. If this behavior came from the one middle-aged guy who didn't open all his exchanges with dick pics and suggestive emojis, what the hell would have greeted me in person if I agreed to meet up with those other men?

I also have a pang of shame as I realize that had this encounter happened 30 years ago, when I was roughly Maddy's age, if I hadn't blown a guy like him off immediately, I likely would've slept with him to be polite and non-confrontational. While a small part of me is proud of myself for not sticking it out on a date that was going terribly, I still have an overwhelming feeling of loneliness and begin to wonder if Dan was my one shot at love in this life.

By the next morning my thoughts of male rejection are replaced by thoughts of job rejection as I receive three similarly written form e-mails from job portals thanking me for my application, but notifying me that they have decided to pursue another candidate more closely aligned with the job. While disappointing at least they didn't call me a chubby cunt Karen.

My phone dings and reminds me that I've scheduled a call with the recruiter that starts in 15 minutes, so I grab a cup of coffee and pull up my resume to make sure I'm prepared to talk about myself coherently. Twenty minutes later I'm staring at my phone wondering if I'm being stood up or if my phone isn't working. I keep unlocking it to make sure it works and begin muttering to myself. Finally, it lights up with an unknown number and I pounce on it like I've just won the lottery.

"Hello this is Jackie!" I announce far too enthusiastically.

"Hi Jackie this is Fiona from Superskills Recruitment, is now still a good time?" she asks. In the background I hear other people talking and typing, as if she works at a call center.

"Hi Fiona, yup, now is still great," I try to calm down.

"Good," she responds. "So, I was looking through your profile and...." she takes a long pause, presumably to look through the LinkedIn profile that she hadn't actually laid eyes on until now. "I'm not exactly sure we have anything that completely aligns with your skills at this exact moment."

"Oh," I say confused. "When you reached out to me last week, I assumed that was because you had a position that could potentially be a fit."

"New positions are coming up all the time," she covers. "But now that we're connected, you are officially in our database and I can reach out as new things come up."

If my date with Javier312 failed because he came on too strong, my phone date with Fiona the recruiter was failing because she came on completely uninterested.

"OK," I say skeptically. "I mean, do you want to ask me any questions about what I'm interested in or my past jobs to help get a better sense of what might be a good fit?"

"Ummm," she stalls over the din of others typing and talking in the background, "I think I have everything I need based on your online profile. Our robust and proprietary AI software will align your skills with jobs that may be a perfect match, so I'll be in touch should anything come up."

"Gotcha," I half laugh. You've got to be kidding me.

"Good luck in your search, and we'll be in touch," she says robotically before hanging up.

If Fiona was on a dating app, her outreach would be the equivalent texting a wide swath of women "Sup" with an enticing emoji.

Disappointed, I get myself together and ride a bus

and the L up to Debbie's. On the train I watch people around me scroll through their phones. I assume that they too are looking at and for the fantasy lives that seem elusive to me. I get off the train, walk down the platform, and am greeted at street level by Debbie in her minivan. I feel a sense of relief in a way that a college student coming home on break feels. For just a little bit of time, I don't need to be in charge of me anymore, someone else can take the wheel.

During the 15-minute drive to her house, I brief Debbie on the conversation with our mother, the job rejections, and the debacle of a date with Javier312. By the time we walk into her house I'm in full-on vent mode just unloading every thought and negative thing that's recently happened to me upon her in great detail.

"And then this guy Freddy from my neighborhood made me buy him booze when I ran into him in Binny's," I add. "Can you believe that?"

"Well," she pauses, "at least you have exciting stuff going on."

"Exciting?" I laugh. "Hardly."

Debbie's house always looks and smells like a HomeGoods store. There are large multi-wicked candles on every flat surface emitting some sort of spicy or citrusy smell, changed out for each season. The throw pillows match the curtains, which align with the colors featured in her latest wall hanging and knickknack. The whole house is "mom-level" clean, a clean that no matter how hard I've tried, I've never been able to achieve. There is never an errant pubic hair near her toilet or old bits of salsa stuck in the kitchen sink. Even the drawers of her fridge are immaculately clean.

"Jackie," she sighs. "You are living, you are experiencing things, you are on the precipice of starting a whole new chapter of your life. Don't you realize how exciting that is?"

Is she insane? "I think I'm on the precipice of falling off a cliff, Debs," I correct. "Or on the verge of moving back in with mom."

"Don't even," she warns. "You can move into Maddy's old room before you move back with mom. Having you live here would be the lesser of the two evils because if you two lived together I'd be getting calls from both of you complaining."

She pulls out a lunch spread that she probably made hours in advance, including a charcuterie platter and an assortment of cold salads as if there would be seven people joining us.

"I'm just saying, Jack," she continues, "that you need to reframe how you look at everything. Yes, things may suck right now, but look at all these new experiences you're having. That to me seems really exciting." She has no idea.

I look at her and realize she seems a bit forlorn and almost sounds a bit … jealous?

"Is everything OK with you?" I ask. I grab a stool at her kitchen island and start picking at the cheese board. "You know I would kill for your life, right? Well, maybe not the whole thing…" I playfully gesture at the wall of inspirational word signs she has hanging in the kitchen that I've made fun of since she hung them up a few years ago.

"I dunno about that," she shakes her head and swats at my arm.

"What do you mean?" I ask sincerely. "Maddy is doing amazing and is like a voice of her generation or something. Cameron is just about to graduate and, yeah, he may not have it all figured out yet, but he'll be fine. Tom is such a good stable guy."

"We haven't had sex in three years," she blurts out. I nearly spit out the flavored seltzer that I just took a gulp of.

"What?" I ask incredulously.

"I don't want your judgment, Jack," she says sternly. "It just is what it is and I just needed to say it out loud."

"But you guys are so good," I plead. "You're Deb and Tom. I mean even when Dan and I were at each other's throats we were still having sex."

"Thanks," she rolls her eyes.

"No, I don't mean it like that," I apologize. "I mean it like, what's happening? Is it hormones or something?"

"I dunno," she says. "Maybe. Things got so hellish during the pandemic with the kids, the fear, worrying about everything, if they were gonna be OK. I think like on one of our regular sex nights I said I was too tired or whatnot and he was cool with it. Then like we just never picked it back up again and now it feels like it's just a thing we don't do anymore. You know like when people stop driving at night or don't go to concerts where it's standing room only. It just sorta happened without realizing it."

"I guess," I add. "But are you OK with that? I mean do you want to be having sex?" I stare at her intensely trying to X-ray a rationale out of her. Was my straightlaced sister who I always thought I knew about to come out as gay? Pan? Or even a-sexual?

"I think I do," she says hesitantly. "Like I think I miss it. But I almost don't know if I still have sexy inside of me, you know? Like the mom me, the caretaker me, and the Debbie of the neighborhood me sort of took over. So, I don't know if sexy me even still exists or even matters."

I'm trying to be conscious of how I'm looking at her. I don't want to give off a face that is in any way judgmental, but my mind is having a Judge Judy marathon playing at triple speed in my head.

"What about Tom?" I ask. "I mean does he ever try to start something?"

"Maybe when we first dropped off," she replies. "But now I think we're just in the same boat. Kinda no one expects anything, so we just get in bed, play with our phones, and then go to sleep. I think he may just watch a lot of porn on his phone because I've caught him turning stuff off when I've gone into a room unannounced."

"I know I'm in no position to offer anyone relationship advice," I hedge.

"No, you're not," she confirms.

"But Deb, if this is something that matters to you, you need to talk to Tom. I mean Cameron's graduating, you guys might be empty nesters soon. Now's finally the time for you two to be Deb and Tom! You know, do what you want, when you want. You could be sexpot nudists around the house if you wanted," I laugh. "You're about to embark on a whole new chapter just as much as I am, so you need to figure out what's in that chapter too."

"I know you think you've cornered the market on fucked up, sad sack behavior," Debbie says. "But you haven't. Everyone has something, Jackie. Yours is just way more out front because you talk about it. The rest of us are out here making everything look fine and dying on the inside."

I walk around the kitchen island as Debbie starts to nearly cry as I give her a big hug. After 30 seconds she waves me off.

"Oh geez," she says. "This is not supposed to be how today goes. I'm supposed to be telling you that everything is going to be OK, not the other way around."

"Debbie," I correct, "it's a two-way street. I got your back. I know it usually goes one way, but it doesn't have to."

"I think I'm just getting emotional, because my time as being a mom is sorta coming to an end and I'm just left with 'who the hell am I now'?," she adds. "Maybe I'm just stressed about planning Cam's graduation party, you know? It's probably just that." She wipes her eyes and puts on a smile that suggests she wants me to ignore everything she just said and pretend everything is fine because that's what she intends to do.

"You can always talk to me Debs. And your life is far from over," I insist. "Maybe after Maddy finishes making me over she can take you on next," I joke.

"Right," she laughs. "Maddy will never see me as anything more than her minivan-driving boring mom. No amount of lipstick and hair extensions will change that up."

"You don't really think that, do you Deb?" I ask. By her face I can tell that she does and that she's also done talking about herself.

"Enough," she says. "I mean it." She starts putting out napkins and rummaging around her kitchen junk drawer for nothing in particular in an effort to change the topic. "That whole date story of yours is wild. I mean that's what I worry about for Mads and Cam, like that will be their whole dating life experience. A bunch of AI powered meet ups with people who pretend to be someone else who think getting together serves the sole purpose of hooking up and never going beyond that."

"I dunno," I add. "I think after doing that for a bit they'll just get burned out and probably take credit for discovering traditional in-person meet and greet dating out of necessity."

As we polish off the cheese plate, I find myself treading lightly as I fill her in on my other complaints and anxieties. This is the first time, in a long time, that I see her as a person whose life isn't perfect. I explain that a team of lawyers is looking into age discrimination case at my former company.

"Jack," she says sternly. "What I've always loved about you, is that your job has never defined who you are. I mean think about Dad or Tom or even Maddy. Their jobs are their whole lives and identity. You always worked to support yourself, but like it was an afterthought. As soon as the clock hit five, you were like Fred Flintstone sliding down the dinosaur's back and off doing something you wanted to. I mean I look at folks who are workaholics and you wonder why they're trying so hard at something that doesn't mean anything.

Like in 20 years is anyone gonna care what makeup Maddy wore or what couch she sat on? No."

"But in 20 years Maddy will have enough savings and investments to do whatever she wants. She won't be sitting around Cam's kitchen wondering how she can go on with her life as a middle-aged broke person," I interject.

"Yeah," Debbie replies. "But will she have really lived? I mean yes you are a divorced middle-aged woman complaining in your hot mess of a sister's kitchen right now wondering where your next paycheck will come from. But my God, Jack, you've lived. You've seen shows, and bands, and theater, you've drank with the best of them and threw up with the worst of them, you've travelled and you had a really good marriage for a while. You have hilarious and incredible stories to show for it. You don't need to go figure out a new life's work. I think you just need to find some kind of work and get on with your life."

I stare at Debbie while her words sink in. For the second time since I arrived, I get up and give her a hug for saying exactly what I needed to hear, but didn't know I needed. In spending so much time looking at social media recently, I think I may have gotten caught up in finding some sort of dream job that would make others swoon. Maybe I'm just living a different dream - one that's peppered with being a waking nightmare.

"Thank you for always setting me straight," I say. "Though I still don't know how I'm going to pay rent the month after next if something doesn't materialize soon."

"Jackie," she says hesitantly, "building on the momentum of setting you straight..." I can see the wheels turning in Debbie's head trying to figure out the best way to spin something negative so that I'll find it palatable. She frequently had the same look on her face when she was a pre-teen and would come into my room to tell me that she borrowed some article of my clothing and then promptly spilled something on it or left it at school.

"Spit it out," I snap.

"Do you really need to be in a full amenity building in a pricey and trendy neighborhood right now?" she asks. "I mean I'm not suggesting you move out to the burbs or into a garage, but maybe when your lease is up you can consider a place that's a little cheaper? It's not like you're 24 and partying every night and checking out all the new bars and restaurants. Maybe just someplace a little quieter and cheaper. And it wouldn't hurt if you didn't, ya know, go out for coffee all the time and get take out for meals. You have that super fancy coffee maker in your kitchen, just make it yourself."

I roll my eyes and shake my head, but recognize that she has a point. This too may be a holdover from my younger years when where you lived and where you ate was significantly more important than what you did.

"Well at this point, no one's going to rent an apartment to someone with no income and limited reserves so I'm sorta stuck there for a bit. I know it was a bit of a knee jerk reaction with the divorce, but I couldn't let Dan win at life and force me out into some far-flung neighborhood."

"I know, I know," she consoles. "But just like I worry about Maddy living too much in a world judged by what everyone thinks, maybe you need to stop doing that to some degree too and start thinking about what's actually practical."

"OK, wise woman," I laugh. "I'll consider it. But you need to promise to consider yourself too. I mean it Debs, I had no idea about any of this and I'm guessing no one else does either. Maybe not even Tom. Speak up. Or for fuck's sake, see a therapist."

She gives me a closed lipped smile and a look that is both kind and condescending, insinuating that she truly wants to stop talking about herself.

"Three weeks to the graduation party, and then I can try to think about me," she says. "Promise."

The rest of the afternoon at Debbie's is more light hearted as we switch to topics less controversial and deep-seated. Nearly an hour is spent recounting conversations that illustrate the ineptitude of our mother, while another hour is spent devoted to various reality television programs that we're ashamed to admit we watch to anyone other than each other.

I head back home before Tom and Cameron return for the evening, replaying Debbie's comments and advice in my head. Maybe she was onto something. Had I set some sort of goal of what a successful life looked like when I was a little kid and never took the time to adjust it? By the time I was 30 I'd hit that goal - cool apartment, cool neighborhood, cool husband, and then I just set it and forget it and never evolved. It pained me to think about it now, but maybe Dan was right all along?

My moment of podcast-level self-reflection is interrupted when a young man gets on the L and lights a joint near the door vestibule. He has a small speaker clipped to his jacket that is blasting music on the otherwise peaceful train. I catch the eye of several fellow passengers who are quick to look away, everyone hoping that this young man just disappears and doesn't start trouble. Just two stops away from home, I stare out of the window trying to get back into my thoughts, as the cloud of his weed wafts over everyone in the train.

In the window I catch his reflection starting directly at me. I must've made a face because the next thing I know he's speaking loudly toward me from across the train.

"I see you staring at me red," he nods his chin up

in my direction. "You never let loose before? Never had no fun? Have you been uptight your whole life or just now?" he laughs.

With one stop to go, I know I can play this one of two ways. The more common and safer bet is to just not react at all. Pretend I have earbuds in and don't hear him, or sit there frozen and repeat the old Pee Wee Herman saying in my head "I'm rubber and you're glue, everything you say bounces off of me and sticks to you." The other riskier way to go is to interact and hope that this kid isn't armed, or getting off at the same stop as me leading to a big altercation.

"Oh what," he continues, "you pretending you can't hear me?"

Debbie's words echoing in my head about my prior fearlessness, mentally embolden me to think about taking the less safe route. My fellow passengers are sitting with their eyes down wondering what I'm going to do probably as much as I'm wondering it myself. This kid is maybe 15 years old and high as a kite, both states I'm exceedingly familiar with. With only about 30 seconds left to my ride, I consider getting up and walking toward him and confronting him about how he's being disrespectful and annoying as fuck to people who are just trying to get where they need to go.

I envision myself making some Liam Neeson-level

badass tough-guy speech that is so eloquent and moving that it makes the kid realize the errors of his ways. My fantasy continues, with fellow train passengers standing up to cheer and clap at me being an everyday hero and asset to the city. Someone will undoubtedly have videoed the whole interaction and within a few hours I'll be a viral sensation that grabs the attention of the mayor's office, which consequently lands me a dream job doing something I'd never even thought of doing.

Unfortunately, this hero fantasy in my head ends up being the equivalent of all my other recent fantasies. Fiction. Rather than getting up and addressing this boy and his issues head on, I instead allow this teenager to yell comments as I stand up and proceed to the other train door at the far side of the car to make sure I avoid confrontation at all costs. I feel like I did in junior high, when I was one of the first girls to develop breasts and all the boys would point and make snickering comments because they didn't know how to react to me. I'd just pretend I didn't hear them or their words didn't seep into the fabric of who I'd become.

The train doors open and the biggest and most badass gesture I can muster is giving him the finger after the doors close and the train is safely pulling away. So much for being brave and bold.

SIX

Midday on Wednesday my phone rings from an unknown number. I wonder if perhaps I got the recruiter all wrong and it's Fiona calling to ask if I'm ready for some dream job that her AI software matched me with.

"Is this Jacqueline Novak?" the person asks.

"This is she," I reply in a manner and tone that I haven't used since I was in the seventh grade when my mother gave me and Debbie formal how-to-answer-the-phone lessons.

"Jacqueline, this is Rhonda Burns from Steinhoff, Bergen, and Johnson, the firm working on the age discrimination case you are a part of. I think you spoke to one of my colleagues," she says.

"Oh my gosh, yes," I say a bit too enthusiastically.

"Right, well we did hear back from your former employer," she says. "Now in your case they actually wanted to change your termination status from layoff due to restructure to firing for cause. They've cited, let me just find it here," she pauses, "use of company provided computer equipment to conduct personal Internet searches and business, return of company issued equipment in poor working condition, failure to show up for work without pre-approved time off, and failure to correctly code your time sheet, as a list of reasons."

"What?" I ask incredulously, "can they do that? Like fire me after I'm already let go?"

"Well, this can be used as a scare tactic when lawsuits come into play. Typically, what they do is just contest your ability to apply for unemployment benefits. Honestly, I know those sound like a bunch of serious accusations, but I assume they are referring to you paying some online bills through your work computer or going to a dentist appointment without marking it on your time sheet," she says. "Am I right?"

"Ya," I agree, my voice screeching at a high octave in an attempt to conceal the fact that I returned the computer wrapped in a dirty t-shirt absorbing water, skipped entire days of work while I cried over my divorce, and used the middle finger emoji as a note for work time that I put on my time sheet.

"Ordinarily I wouldn't even come to you with this, but there actually was a bit of a twist in what they came back with. Despite saying all this stuff, they want to offer you contract work," she says. "Now what this suggests to me is that they laid you and the others off, but now that they've had a few weeks to work without you they are now panicking because not only are you all suing them, but they now realize they can't deliver their work without you."

"So let me get this straight, they're mad that I'm part of this lawsuit, so they threaten to cut off my unemployment benefits and say they fired me for cause, but that if I want to, I can come back as a contractor and do the work I was doing before without benefits or job security?" I laugh.

"Yes," she says. "And I'll also add that if you were to agree to that, you would be forfeiting your rights to be part of the discrimination suit. So, if we do end up settling, you wouldn't be entitled to any compensation from that."

"That sounds crazy," I blurt.

"Well, it's entirely up to you," she says monotone. "I'm not sure what the job market is like for your profession and what your financial situation is. For some people, while it may be a bit of a blow to their ego to go back to someplace that is behaving in this way, it makes the most financial sense. For others, they might decide they wouldn't go back to that place for a million dollars and prefer to see what the lawsuit brings. I need to remind you that a payout from a lawsuit is in no way guaranteed."

My knee jerk reaction to say "fuck them, burn it to the ground," changes quite drastically after hearing the rest of her speech. She provides a contractor rate that they offer to pay with a guarantee of 30 hours per week. I would need to sign a one-year contract.

"You don't have to decide right now, you can think about it," she says. "They have given a deadline of end of day Friday to respond. If you can let us know by mid-day Friday, that would be great."

"Thank you for running through this for me," I respond.

"No problem," she says. "And Jacqueline, a little bit of unsolicited off the record advice. This happens all the time. There is no shame in going back to a company, if that's what you decide to do. You need to remember that companies are not people, so it's not like getting back together with an ex-spouse or something like that. They let you go because a number cruncher decided that was the best thing to do, and they are asking you back because some different number cruncher made a different decision. You need to be your own number cruncher and see what works best for you."

"Thank you for that, Rhonda, I appreciate it."

I hang up the phone and am more confused than when I started. I would rather stick needles in my eyes than have to once again deal with the bosses who so smugly fired me. On the other hand, I've gotten absolutely no traction on the job front and could be couch surfing at Debbie's or my mother's within a few months if something doesn't materialize soon. At the very least I need to think about paying for health insurance which will soon be coming to an end.

I'd texted Liz a few times to find out how things were going at Reed Publishing and she said it was a shitshow over there. If I went crawling back, it would at least be returning to the devil I know. A devil that laid me off, then fired me, and then asked me back. But as a contractor, I wouldn't necessarily be as involved in the day-to-day madness as I was as a full-time employee. That said, money would be tighter given the reduced hours, the need to pay my own employment taxes, and my own healthcare costs. At the very least if things got unbearable or something better came along, I could potentially figure out a way to break my contract and leave them in the lurch like they had done to me.

Smack in the middle of the situation I'm unable to see it clearly. Therefore, I decide to procrastinate on the decision until Friday morning. Maybe tomorrow's day out with Maddy will be better than I hope and I'll leave looking like a new woman who people will stop in the street offering six figure sponsorship deals. More likely, I will just be the same woman with a new haircut now known as a freelance editor, but a girl can dream.

❖ ❖ ❖

On Thursday I hide any unmentionables in the apartment in preparation for Arlo and Riff to come ransack it unsupervised and work their invisible magic. I head down to Maddy's loft where we're slated to have our makeover day. She tells me to leave my phone off for the day to truly get an immersive experience. I told her that that would be no problem as I typically forget it anyway and make the conscious decision to leave it at home, a concept she finds both horrifying and unthinkable.

When I arrive, it's clear that Janelle calls the shots in Maddy's life ushering her around like she's a publicist or handler for a massive celebrity. While Maddy chit chats and has someone do her makeup and hair, Janelle is juggling two cell phones while also giving secret hand and eye signals to Maddy's "glam squad" to hurry things along. As they finish up with her, I move over and prepare to hop in the chair that she vacates.

"You guys are amazing," I say to the team. "Can't wait to see what you do with me!" They look at each other slightly confused and then turn back toward Janelle for guidance.

"Aunt Jack," Maddy pipes up, "this is my glam squad, silly. They aren't going to be working on you. This will be more, you know, relatable content for regular people attached to some sponsored deals. So, we'll go to a local salon for hair, Makeup Mecca for makeup and skincare, and then I think, correct me if I'm wrong Janelle, but did Fashion Finds send over stuff for Jackie?"

Janelle nods and points to the corner of the office area in Maddy's loft which looks like a package room in a large apartment building. She must have nearly every company that one sees advertised online sending her things to promote or review. Most of it sits unopened, likely awaiting a monetary decision on how much Maddy will get paid for even looking at it.

"Ya, so it's this AI powered company that picks clothes for you and you can try them on at home and only buy what you want. I think they sent over more than the standard number of pieces for you to try based on the profile Janelle created for you," she explains. "So, after Makeup Mecca, we'll come back here, do a little fashion show and then you and I can take a car back to your place and do the apartment update reveal." My mind tries to take this all in, but I get hung up on the fact that Janelle, who met me once, has somehow created a profile for me.

"You have four hours," Janelle reminds Maddy.

"Four hours to do all that?" I ask.

"It'll be fine aunt Jackie," Maddy reassures. "The MadLove team is amazing. We'll have our intern

Xyla with us today filming so it will help make everything go that much faster and smoother."

I look over to see a person who looks to be about twelve years old wearing a crop top that says "Glue" on it and a pair of bike shorts sitting next to Janelle. If this is what the modern workplace looks like, I understand why I may not be first on the list of callbacks when applying to jobs.

Maddy's glam squad finishes up with her and Maddy looks supremely pleased with the results. I see my beautiful niece looking like she now belongs on an episode of RuPaul's *Drag Race* covered in thick contouring makeup that would turn a white towel into the Shroud of Turin if she wiped her face on it. Her actual hair is entangled with nearly waist-length extensions that she can't stop herself from playing with and her eyelashes are so long I am confused about how she can wear the designer sunglasses Janelle hands her without them repeatedly touching the lenses.

"It takes a village," she laughs as she sees me staring at her. "It's all a masterful illusion." I smile not letting on that my thoughts were those of astonishment not admiration. I brace myself for what type of illusion I'll end up with by the end of the day.

Maddy, Janelle, Xyla and I head out to a waiting SUV with tinted windows and spacious rows of seats. While they barely acknowledge the driver or the fanciness of the vehicle, on the inside I'm secretly behaving like a 1980s high school senior who is going to prom and gets to see the inside of a limousine for the first time. Whenever I order an Uber or Lyft, I typically end up waiting for a Toyota Prius to arrive with stained back seats and hideous autotune music blaring loud enough to shake the back windows. This was truly seeing how the other half lives and the other half apparently live non-plussed by their fortunate circumstances.

We arrive at a Salon called Hair Dares about 15 minutes later. Before we walk in Maddy and Janelle position me under the salon's sign, Xyla pulls out a camera with a fuzzy little boom mic on the top and points at Maddy to look at the lens.

"Hey MadLovers," Maddy starts talking to the camera, "I'm here at Hair Dares with Jackie, my favorite aunt, who you may remember from my Insta live last week. We are going to have the folks at Hair Dares work their Mad Magic to transform Jackie's look into the current century and help jump start the next chapter in her life. Stay tuned to see how it all turns out."

Maddy delivers this well-spoken intro as if she's a field reporter teasing an upcoming segment about a world-changing story. She's poised and articulate and came alive with barely a heads up or any type of cue. Meanwhile the whole time that Maddy's speaking, I stand there looking like an idiot with a smile plastered on my face as if someone was counting down to tell me to say cheese for a picture. Janelle instructs Maddy to do another take for a YouTube intro so they have options on where to place it, and without missing a beat Maddy repeats the same intro except this time adds a line about liking and subscribing. I believe I had the same deer-in-the-headlights expression on my face in the second take that I did in the first.

"Jackie can you please hold a neutral expression and then just slowly turn in a complete circle to your right?" Janelle asks. "Xyla is just gonna get some B roll for the before shot of your hair. We'll also do some once you're in the chair, but the lighting out here is looking really good." Out of my depth I stand there trying to process what she's saying. I feel like I do when the mammogram tech tells me to move to the right and left and hold all sorts of awkward positions. I find myself struggling to follow simple directions because I'm overexposed and out of sorts.

"Arms out, and spin slowly," Janelle repeats, demonstrating herself, with a tone that would be more appropriately used on a dog one is trying to potty train.

I do as I'm told and can only compare it to the opening sequence of the reality show *Naked and Afraid* where some unprepared amateur survivalist is shown spinning in a circle as their skillset is read aloud by a narrator. At the end they give them a score about how well they are predicted to survive in the woods without clothes, tools, or food. At the moment, my predicted score of surviving this makeover just plummeted to whatever numerically converts to "not likely."

We walk into the salon and Xyla films Maddy and I meeting with Darwin, one of the lead stylists at the salon. Darwin is a tall strikingly handsome young Black man who is wearing a long plaid skirt, form fitting black turtleneck, and combat boots. He has a septum piercing and eyes that seem to see into your soul. Darwin introduces us to Crystal, a young perky blonde woman who will be filming today's interaction on behalf of the salon for their social media. She seems to be fangirling out at the sight of Maddy and I beam with pride watching Maddy being so kind to her.

As they talk angles and lighting, I look around and realize that Hair Dares is a little less daring than I'd expected. Living in an edgier neighborhood, I've grown accustomed to seeing everyone with at least one part of their head shaved, dyed a primary color, or cut into an ironic mullet. The clientele and pictures featured on the "Inspiration Wall" of this salon seem to all feature variations of the same long hair with one wave crimped around shoulder height, popular among the young social media savvy set.

I catch Maddy waving me over out of the corner of my eye and I sit down in the designated chair. She and Janelle let me know that they'll be filming the whole time to do some time lapse takes and that I should just act as naturally as possible through the whole process. I smile nervously and shake my head in agreement knowing that when the camera is pointed at me, I will be acting in a way that is anything but natural.

"So," Darwin winks. He starts brushing and playing with my hair making it look big and unkempt and rubbing it between his fingers. "What are we looking to do today, Jackie? I love the red. I'm thinking deepening that a little and adding length to give some Julianne Moore vibes." Crystal nods her head up and down as both she and Xyla film me in the mirror at an angle that ensures they aren't visible on camera.

"Wow, interesting," I say. "I love Julianne Moore, but I'm not sure that's really who I am. I'm actually kind of digging the gray stripe that is coming in in the front. Sorta a Bonnie Raitt vibe?" The moment the words leave my lips I realize that my dated reference would be met with confusion.

"I don't know who that is," Darwin says sincerely. I mentally run through my other female heroes sporting a gray stripe and realize that Mrs. Robinson and the Bride of Frankenstein may also be met with a perplexed response. "Well, I guess, I mean, just sorta the two-tone effect," I continue. "I know myself. I really can't be bothered with keeping up with color maintenance. I'm also thinking of going a bit shorter, maybe like a shoulder length bob? So, something like that?" I smile excitedly. Darwin's face drops.

"Um MADDY?" Darwin yells slightly panicky while still looking at the mirror. Maddy had moved across the salon and was sitting against a back wall typing furiously on her phone. She walks over when summoned. "Maddy, did you tell Jackie about the extensions?"

"Oh, no, I'm so sorry Darwin," she says. "I totally spaced. Jack, Darwin's amazing team is promoting a new line of extensions that they've created. You probably saw them on the inspiration wall over there, they're fab. So as part of this collab they're gonna feature them in your hair makeover."

"Oh," I say taken aback. "Congrats on the new line, Darwin. But I don't really want extensions as much as I appreciate the offer. I just want, you know, a more modern cut, something low maintenance."

I just told the man that I couldn't be bothered keeping up with hair dye, there is no way I'm walking out of this salon with fake hair intertwined with my own.

Darwin's welcoming and warm look shifts and he gives Maddy a "really?" glare that results in the two of them stepping away from me out of earshot. Janelle joins them and they are embroiled in a heated and huddled discussion that seems more on par with negotiating a corporate merger than a haircut. Darwin and Janelle remain in the corner as Maddy breaks away to approach me.

"Aunt Jack?" she half whispers. "So, here's the deal. Darwin is the best and he's normally booked up, like months in advance and charges like what you probably pay in rent for a haircut. Arlo was able negotiate a sponsored partnership content deal with him to help revamp your look, but it only works if you have extensions put in. He's about to start launching the collection at Ultimate Beauty and this is a really crucial part of his go-to-market strategy and getting the word out."

"I think that's great for him, Mads," I whisper back. "But I'm not a hair extensions type of person. I'm 52, not 25. I'm potentially going out for job interviews and what not and don't want to look like I'm auditioning to be on the *Real Housewives of Chicago*." She thinks for a minute and then leans in again.

"Would you be willing to do clip in extensions?" she asks. Her demeanor changes and I feel myself being managed like an employee who refuses to follow the latest new work process. "I think I can get him to agree to that. Those are no commitment. He could give you a haircut and then incorporate those and you would have all of today's content filmed with them in and then you can take them out later if you wanted."

Fucking hell. "That sounds fine, Maddy," I agree, snarling on the inside. "Thank you for working that out."

They regroup in the huddle and I see Maddy working her magic to convince Darwin this is the best option for everyone. I can't make out what they're saying, but by body language alone I can tell that this is definitely not an easy conversation to have and Darwin is no longer as thrilled as he was when we came in. They break up their group and Darwin comes back toward me forcing a smile. Crystal and Xyla retake their positions and Darwin nods his head to them to start filming.

"So, Jackie," he says, playing with my hair in the same manner he had started to before. "What would you think about keeping it natural, I'm really liking this gray stripe you have coming in, in contrast to your red. Then for a cut, a few face framing layers to showcase those big blue eyes, a shoulder length bob for the rest. And then to do something really special, which you can replicate yourself at home, adding in some clip-in extensions from the Darwinian Hair Dares collection that I'm launching in partnership with Ultimate Beauty?"

"That sounds great," I say stiffly, quickly glancing at the two cameras being pointed at through me through the mirror. "I really appreciate anything and trust your judgement."

Darwin steps out of frame to go prepare for the cut and Xyla and Crystal circle around me with their cameras as I hold a pained neutral expression akin to when the mammogram technician ultimately tells me to hold my breath as they flatten my breasts into pancakes. When Darwin returns, I'm spun around so my back is to the mirror and the two cameras are set up on tripods to record time lapse video. At this point Darwin seems to be annoyed by me, so I take it as a cue to just be quiet and let him do his thing. He puts in discreet earbuds and begins taking phone calls while simultaneously whipping through cutting my hair like a montage scene in the film *Edward Scissorhands*. Swaths of hair fly all over the chair and floor and I'm slightly fearful he's cutting it all off and will just place a wig on my head at the end out of spite.

He wets my hair and puts some product in it and then starts blow drying it with extreme force so that my head jerks from one side to the other. Once done, he brings over a cart that has several clips of long red hair on it. He holds up a few trying to find the perfect shade of red and then begins clipping them in near my scalp with the finesse of someone who is stapling flyers to a telephone pole. Too afraid to make a joke or ask if he could maybe be a bit softer, I sit there trying to keep a neutral expression on my face.

Darwin steps back to look at me. He steps forward and does a little messing around with product and then steps back once again. He pulls his earbuds out and summons Maddy back over along with Janelle and Crystal.

"OK Jackie," Janelle explains. "We're going to spin you around in a minute after an intro and we need you to get ready to react. So, lots of energy, OK?"

"I'm ready!" I say a little too loudly trying to get the team to change any opinion they have of me being difficult into something more positive.

"Ok, MadLovers," Maddy starts. "We're ready to reveal Jackie's amazing new hair thanks to Darwin and his team's fabulous work. He's incorporated Darwin's Hair Dares line of extensions which you can exclusively find at Ultimate Beauty and I swear even I'm a bit jealous of how she looks."

Darwin spins me around and for the first time I'm able to see myself in the mirror. I nearly do a double take.

"It's like if the Little Mermaid got old," I laugh out loud.

"JACKIE!" Maddy scolds.

I couldn't help myself. I honestly looked like I was partially getting ready for a Halloween party as the Little Mermaid's mom. While I had my gray stripe up front, I had cascading voluminous red hair extensions coming down to my elbows. I just looked comical. Darwin didn't see it this way and seemed like he was about to wrap the extensions around my neck.

"I'm so sorry," I apologize and try to walk back my sincere reaction. "I'm just not used to seeing myself this way. Can I have a minute to get used to it and then we film the reaction again? Darwin, I really appreciate everything you've done. I just am not used to change, let alone one this drastic, so I think I'm just masking my discomfort with inappropriate humor."

Maddy shoots me a look that reflects that I'm trying her patience and Darwin shoots Maddy a look that suggests I'm trying to ruin him. I shoot them both a look that I'm just simply trying. They agree to reshoot the reaction sequence, and I attempt to bring a sense of gratitude and enthusiasm.

"Oh my GOD," I yell somewhat stiffly as I look at myself in the mirror and try not to laugh. "This is AMAZING Darwin, thank you so much. I could never imagine I could look like this." All truth, but perhaps just not the truth they were hoping for. I plaster a smile on my face that looks like I'm being held up at gunpoint. Realizing that this is the best they're going to get out of me, Darwin and Maddy start speaking to their audiences and highlight all the proprietary products they used to create my look.

The session wraps up soon after with Maddy kissing Darwin and him wishing me the best of luck with my new look, probably realizing that his coveted hair extensions will be thrown into the bottom of my closet the moment I get home, only to be whipped out as drunken party costumes at some later date. I thank him profusely and once again apologize for my immediate and unexpected reaction.

When Maddy, Janelle, Xyla, and I get into the new SUV that's waiting for us, Maddy once again scolds me akin to how my mother would wait to yell at Debbie and I for some public indiscretion until we were out of earshot of others.

"Aunt Jack," she says, "I know this whole world is new to you, but you really need to try to get on board with it. You can't be making fun of our sponsor's products or their services."

"I know, I know, Mads," I apologize again. "But come on, these extensions are just so…" I start flipping my hair behind my back in a mock Cher drag queen move that amuses no one but myself. "I'll be better with the next one, I promise."

As we drive to our next destination, Xyla previews some of the video she took through the camera's screen to Janelle and Maddy. I sit in the second row of seats in the SUV quietly behaving like a toddler who was just told to sit, be quiet, and not touch anything.

A few moments later we pull in front of Makeup Mecca and get out of the car. Once again Xyla starts to film and Maddy seamlessly starts talking like a news reporter sent to cover an important scene. The salon had been on a block where there wasn't a lot of foot traffic, so while odd, I didn't feel self-conscious about filming. However now draped in fake hair and hanging out with a group of people thirty years my junior standing in front of a popular and highly populated Makeup Mecca store I feel like all eyes are staring at me with a combination of curiosity and disdain. I'd personally encountered influencers filming themselves at spots around town and rolled my eyes, walked through their shot, or muttered something unkind in their direction.

When Maddy stops speaking, a group of young women approach her and ask if they could have selfies with her. She enthusiastically obliges and once again I am taken aback by how many strangers know her and think so highly of her. All of my celebrity references are at least 30 years old and other than my own niece I couldn't name another social media influencer if I tried.

Standing there, I feel both a sense of awe for all she's accomplished and a sense of irrelevancy in that the world that I am so familiar with is rapidly becoming no more. Even covered in long fake red hair I'm invisible to these young people mesmerized by a young woman selling herself as a product. Janelle politely and expertly extracts Maddy from her fans and ushers us all into Makeup Mecca for the next step in the makeover process.

Inside, I meet Anastasia who will be doing my

makeup. She is roughly six feet tall, svelte, with honey blonde hair cascading down her back, wearing the tiniest black dress showing off her endless legs. Her makeup is so thick that it reminds me of the exaggerated stage makeup that my mother would apply on Debbie and me when we were in elementary school dance recitals. Her lips are slightly inflated and her face doesn't move when she speaks, giving her that slightly blow-up-doll-esque appearance that many women have nowadays where you can't tell if they're 20 or 60 years old or even human.

"Look at all these freckles," Anastasia says when looking at my face. Since her face doesn't move or express emotion, I'm unsure if the comment is meant to be tinged with disdain or admiration.

"I'm the only redhead in the family," I confess with a small laugh. "Putting on some sunscreen and bright lipstick is pretty much the extent of my makeup routine. I don't even think I put much more than that on at my wedding."

"I have something that can cover them," she responds under her breath, confirming that she viewed my freckles as a problem, not a positive attribute.

Similar to the experience at the Hair Dares salon, Maddy records an intro as Xyla circles me to capture my pre-made-up face. Within minutes Anastasia is dabbing my face with liquids, creams, and tapping and blending things on me like I'm a hole in a sheetrock wall in need of spackling and repair.

"This serum is part of our latest plant-based, sustainable line and is great for adding deep tissue moisture and erasing those crow's feet," she says to the camera. "And see how she has all these little bumps and dark circles under her eyes? This liquid formulation will help address those."

She applies moisturizer to my neck, telling me to make sure I apply my sunscreen in an upward motion to both my neck and hands because those are the spots that always reveal someone's true age. I look down at my slightly chubby hands that, to me, still look like they did in back in high school. Perhaps in my case they reveal my emotional age, not a physical one.

Anastasia keeps telling me to look up, look left, close my eyes, pout, smile, stop smiling, and turn away as she dissects my appearance to the camera. It is the equivalent of having a very judgmental dental hygienist criticize my brushing and flossing methodology as if her critical words are actually going to make me change my oral care rituals in my fifties.

With Xyla circling me and Maddy's presence generating a small buzz, everyone walking by the makeup chair keeps looking at me to see if I'm some sort of celebrity. When I'm able to catch their eyes, I can see their curiosity wane when instead of someone nationally famous they instead see a panicky middle-aged woman.

After about a half an hour of pasting and spackling later, Anastasia announces that Maddy and the team can prepare filming for the big reveal. I can tell she's pleased with her work, solely by the fact that she's showing teeth since her forehead and the rest of her face continues to reflect no emotions.

Janelle talks to Xyla about camera angles as Maddy sidles up to me and whispers out of earshot of Anastasia.

"Let's not do a repeat of the hair reaction, Jack," she says. "Whatever you think, you need to come at this with being super happy. You want to particularly love the sustainability serum and what it does for your skin. Ok?" She gives me a look like a parent warning a child to be good at the dinner table of a fancy restaurant. I give her an apologetic look and touch her arm to assure her I'll behave like a grownup.

The team gets into place, Maddy gives an intro, and Anastasia spins me around to face the mirror. I take a breath to take it all in, but that is nearly impossible to do.

"Oh my God," I mutter. I catch Maddy out of the corner of my eye and quickly change my facial expression from horror to a pained smile like I'd just opened a terribly offensive Christmas present but am trying not to offend the gift giver. "It's such a...change."

My face looks like one of those optical illusion murals on the side of a building. My actual skin and features have been erased into a blank canvas on top of which a whole new face has been painted. A face with cheekbones in a different position than my own, fake tanned skin that makes my ears look like they belong to a person of a different ethnicity, and my eyes are now framed in a way that makes them look like a big-eyed painting. She's used a plumping serum on my lips that has caused a burning sensation resulting in the look of eating too much spicy food. There is not a freckle to be found and I worry that if I move my mouth too much visible cracks might form down the front of my nose like a stucco building experiencing an earthquake.

"The sustainable plant-based serum really makes a difference," I manage to say without laughing.

"Right?" Anastasia agrees without irony. "It's a total transformation."

"How about that MadLovers? Jackie looks like a completely different person," Maddy pipes up. "You're a true artist Anastasia. I encourage all viewers to go out to their local Makeup Mecca and find your own Anastasia and check out the amazing products in the new sustainability line to transform your look."

As soon as Xyla stops filming and the large ring light shining on my face goes dark, Anastasia loses all interest in me. She grabs Maddy and her team to take some photos in front of the line of products that the store wants to promote. Without my phone in hand, I can only sit around and watch from the sidelines rather than text gossip to Debbie or zone out on social media like I typically would. Sitting here, real life seems to move excruciatingly slow.

Maddy and the team finally part ways with the Makeup Mecca employees and I'm once again ushered into an awaiting car. When the door closes, the team starts muttering about some future Makeup Mecca deal and sitting there like the emperor wearing no clothes, I can hold my tongue no longer.

"Is anyone going to say anything about how ridiculous I look?" I laugh. "I mean come on, I look like I'm either about to enter the witness protection program or go host a drag brunch!" The three young women look at me stone-faced as if they hadn't noticed that anything was amiss.

"What are you talking about, Jackie?" Maddy says earnestly. "I think you look great."

"Yeah," Janelle adds, "she did a great job with contouring, you don't have a double chin anymore."

Their comments make me grimace and come to the realization that they think looking this way is a good thing. Their beauty ideal is a Kardashian or other internet celebrity who my eyes can't seem to distinguish from another internet celebrity. Meanwhile if they were to look at my social media algorithm, they would dive knee deep into what I assume they would consider imperfections. The people I tend to follow are what my counterparts would've called an alternative crowd, who I find interesting based on the art they create, words they write, or non-mainstream lives they seem to live. My feed is filled with those who have tattoos, partially shaved heads, natural faces, shockingly bright lipstick, gap teeth, a few extra pounds, all wearing vintage and one-of-a-kind clothing that makes them stand out for being unique.

"Don't you guys worry about being, I dunno, like not individuals?" I ask earnestly. No one even looks up. "Maddy, since I don't have my phone, do me a favor and take a photo of me and text it to your mom. I want to see what she says." I'm constantly unsticking my long fake hair from my now slightly burning sticky lips covered in gloss.

"FINE," she agrees, "but you're being dramatic. You'll see, I'm sure she thinks you look great."

"We'll see," I laugh. "And tell her it's not a filter, I really look like this."

Maddy takes the photo and sends it off to Debbie

and I sit in the back still feeling like a pouty teenager whose mother took me to the mall and made me look a way I didn't want to look. Within a minute or two Maddy gets a phone alert.

"She says to tell you to be nice," she conveys.

"See, I told you," I reply vindicated. "That's her way of saying, 'I know it looks crazy but I should be nice to you.'"

"Well, you can try following her advice," Maddy snaps back.

The rest of the car ride is completed in silence and we approach Maddy's apartment to finish the personal makeover portion of the day with new clothes before going back to my apartment to see how Riff and Arlo have transformed it.

Outside of Maddy's apartment building, I'm once again told to spin around in a slow circle while the light is good to capture the hideousness of the outfit I dared to put together myself before being reclothed in God-knows-what. I'm wearing a pair of jeans and black t-shirt that is the shade of black that happens after about 3,000 cycles of washing and drying. While I know it may not be the best I can look, it doesn't feel like it should be thrown in a dumpster either.

Back up in the apartment Maddy does a brief intro on camera for Fashion Finds, the AI driven subscription service that's provided me clothing to try. Janelle directs me to take a large package of clothes into Maddy's bedroom and start trying things on and come out and show the group. Janelle had inputted a profile for me into the site, which supposedly described my current style, my desired style, and some demographic and sizing information.

I dump the contents of the package onto the bed and immediately realize that this AI program must've gotten me confused with someone else. The package contains three crop tops, a neon-colored fanny pack, high waisted button-fly jeans, an ethereal-looking flowered strapless maxi dress, and a jean jacket that had the word Namaste embroidered on the back. I don't even know where to begin. What kind of characteristics had Janelle inputted into this profile?

Remembering Debbie's words to be nice and a good sport, I put on the jeans, crop top and for good measure throw on the fanny pack. I am pleasantly surprised that the jeans actually zip up all the way when I put them on. However, when I look down at the tag dangling from my waistband, I realize that the junior-level sizing has so many Xs in front of the L label that it nearly runs onto 2 different lines. Clearly the good fit does not reflect some magical weight loss on my part. I don't even bother looking in the mirror before I step outside.

"WOW, ISN'T THIS GREAT," I say loudly, stiffly, and sarcastically. "Thank you so much Fashion Find! I hope we can incorporate AI into every aspect of our lives."

The team looks at me and for the first time today I think they actually see the same insanity that I've been seeing with every other step of this makeover process.

"Mads," I continue as all attempts at filming have stopped, "I think this company got my wardrobe mixed up. Half the clothes look like they might belong to Ilana from *Broad City* and the others are very Florence and the Machine. I'm either gonna attend a hippie drum circle gathering or a retro rave. I'm gonna look like shit at either one. I don't think they understand that a 52-year-old doesn't want to be a 22-year-old."

"OK OK!!!" Maddy says, fed up. "You WIN Jackie. This was all a big mistake! Forget it. I'm sorry I tried to do something nice for you."

Xyla and Janelle stare at Maddy, clearly having never seen her display this level of emotion before. They both seem triggered and overwhelmed and unsure of what to do.

"Calm down, Maddy," I say non plussed having dealt with overflowing emotions all my life. "I'm just joking with you. I mean you have to admit that I look utterly ridiculous. Also why is this company even making these types of clothes? I feel like it's the kind of thing you can wear once and it will disintegrate off your body by the time you go to put on your pajamas. Isn't Gen Z all woke about climate change and stuff? Why would anyone buy this fast fashion crap?"

Maddy is still unable to regain her composure, and is now so angry that she can barely speak. Realizing that it may all have gone too far, I take my cue that it's my turn to be the adult for the day.

"Hey, Mads," I touch her back and she flinches away from me like she used to do when she was a young child when I would try to console her when she was having a tantrum. "I'm sorry. I didn't mean to imply these shitty clothes were remotely your fault. I just think it's funny that some robot thinks that this is how anyone should dress, particularly an unemployed woman in her fifties attempting to look her best to get a job. I didn't mean it to be a slight at you if that's how you took it."

"I just have a lot on my shoulders aunt Jack," she says teary eyed.

"I know you do honey," I console. "Why don't we do this. It's been a long day. Let's me and you go back to my apartment. You can take some video and I promise to have a big happy reaction when I walk in. Then we can get some take-out and have dinner at my place like old times, OK? Thank you for all you've done today. I mean it. Let's just go home and have a nice chat and eat slightly garbage-y food. How does that sound?"

Maddy doesn't answer, but shakes her head up

and down. I look over at Janelle and Xyla who are seeing their boss have a meltdown while I'm finally getting to once again see the sensitive little girl I've known her whole life.

"Guys," I say, "thank you so much for today. I really mean that even if I didn't seem like it at first. I just, you know, use humor sometimes to defuse situations where I'm uncomfortable and this whole world is a little uncomfortable for me. But I think you all are amazing. I think Maddy and I will handle the last phase of makeover Thursday ourselves and meet Riff and Arlo up at my apartment. You've really been fantastic with me today and I can't wait to see how it turns out."

They both ignore me and look at Maddy as if they expect her to send out a distress signal that she needs rescuing from this mean, style-less woman who has broken her.

"Thanks guys," Maddy adds. "I think I'm just having a rough week and need a little downtime to take care of my mental health. I'll be all set by tomorrow morning. I promise. Appreciate you!" She holds up heart hands and it takes every fiber of my being to not make a comment about how annoying I find that gesture having faced so many insecure heart-hand emojis at work.

I call us an Uber for the ride up to my apartment and unlike the previous rides of the day, we are met by a car held together with duct tape, that smells like cigarettes and weed, and a bass-heavy soundtrack that is destined to blow out our eardrums by the time our ride is over. Once we get in the car, Maddy is once again camera ready, always prepared in case one of her adoring fans might recognize her. Ahmed, our driver, is not one of her fans so I immediately see her face relax and rest for the 15-minute ride to my apartment.

"I'm just gonna film with my phone if that's OK with you," she says as we approach my apartment door. "We can always come back tomorrow to shoot some B-roll if we need to, but I think we're both just a bit done at the moment, yeah?"

"Fine by me," I agree. She picks up her phone and aims it at me, pointing her finger to start talking. "Can't wait to see what they've done!" I say like I was a TV presenter introducing a big reveal.

SEVEN

I open my apartment door with a big smile plastered on my face determined to look happy for the camera no matter what I'm faced with behind the front door. Despite my best efforts, that smile is immediately replaced with a dropped jaw.

There are towels all over the floor, Arlo is crying in the corner, and Riff is consoling him. My building manager is in the kitchen, part of the kitchen cabinet is removed, and people in workmen outfits are kneeling down on the ground talking, looking into the cabinet.

"What the fuck is going on?!" I yell.

"Maddy!!!" Arlo jumps up and goes over to hug Maddy who looks as stunned as I do.

"Jackie," Riff says far too calmly, "it's all under control now. We just had a little incident."

"There she is!" Brian O'Brien's booming voice

comes into the room behind me. I spin around and he half recoils. "Jesus, Jackie, you look…." In the chaos I'd forgotten that I still was sporting my day's makeover attire, complete with crop top and fanny pack.

"Like if someone embalmed the Little Mermaid and dragged her to Coachella 40 years later against her will?"

"I was gonna say…different," he started to laugh loudly. "But you're not wrong. What the hell happened?"

"You go first," I say taking off the fanny pack and throwing it in the corner of the room.

"Well, when these fine folks were rearranging your apartment, they started the dishwasher and then went out for a little coffee break," he says coyly.

"Fuck," I sigh and apologetically direct my conversation towards Riff and a crumpling Arlo, "I forgot to tell you not to run the dishwasher."

"Ya," Brian responds. "So they came back to a nice little water feature all over your kitchen and living room floor and the woman downstairs who never seems to be home when she's supposed to be, was of course home and having her own water feature in her kitchen from the ceiling."

"We tried calling you," the blank-faced young woman from the apartment management company says. "But we didn't get an answer."

"I left my phone here," I say pointing to it laying on the table. "My niece was giving me a makeover today and wanted me to be mentally present for the day so she asked me to leave it behind. And to answer your question," directing my comment to Brian, "today Maddy proved it's impossible to turn a 52-year-old into a 25-year-old." I moved my hands in a Vanna White motion suggesting a big reveal.

"I can see that," Brian once again laughs. "Pleased to meet you Maddy," he waves.

"So, is this easy to fix?" I ask bracing for the answer.

"Plumbing wise," Brian says, "not a problem. We had to cut through the downstairs ceiling, Marco is down there now finishing up with that, and basically just refit a pipe where there was a loose joint. So that was what was causing the original leak. Since that's fixed, I'm just gonna go ahead and fully reconnect your dishwasher. But in terms of the drywall and stuff…."

"We'll need the name and contact of your renter's insurance company," the management company woman says. They can figure it out in conjunction with Ms. Hofstetter's company downstairs."

"Renter's insurance," I mutter under my breath knowing full well I never purchased any when I moved in. Maddy is now standing next to me looking at the hole and mess in the kitchen.

"I'll cover the cost," she says. "We can put it

through my business insurance since it happened as part of content creation."

I reach over and hug Maddy so hard that she releases a small involuntary gasping noise.

"Eww, aunt Jackie, stop," she demands, pushing me away. "I think our stomach skin touched."

I pull away and start laughing and for the first time have an opportunity to look at the apartment beyond the chaos in the kitchen. All of my boxes that had been piled up in various spots around the perimeter are gone and their contents are tastefully displayed on new shelves. One of the white walls adjacent to my bed has been painted dark green. Arlo and Riff framed several of my favorite band t-shirts, hiding the bits that were torn or stained within the frames. The piles of papers and books that I had strewn about are neatly organized near a little desk area they created in the corner by the TV cabinet. Beautiful curtains that have a green stripe in them to match the accent wall are hung up over the big windows. These were an elegant solution to the afternoon sun, particularly since the only solution I'd managed to come up until this point was to wear sunglasses indoors or randomly tape pieces of paper to the offending spot in the window when I was particularly bothered.

I step into the bathroom that now smells like some fancy artisanal home store and see new matching towels, a fluffy bathmat, and expensive-looking soaps and lotions on the shelves. When I exit, I nearly have tears in my eyes, as does Arlo who still can't seem to fathom that his actions flooded my apartment.

"Group hug, you three," I say genuinely. "You knocked it out of the park with the apartment. I mean you also knocked down my neighbor's ceiling, but design-wise it's just lovely."

I embrace Arlo, Riff, and Maddy who all seem reluctant to hug, but I force it upon them anyway.

"I think your stomach skin just touched my arm," Riff says laughing.

"This is all Maddy's fault," I blame, "she should know better than to put a grown-ass woman in a crop top."

"I'm so sorry about the water," Arlo goes on.

"Don't worry about it," I console. "It was my fault that I didn't tell you about the dishwasher. Plus, it's always a good excuse to see Brian, I hadn't seen him in like a week." I look over and Brian winks at me. "I mean it though, the apartment looks great. I look like a mess, but the apartment looks great."

As clean up and plumbing continue over the next hour, Arlo and Riff eventually leave having certainly done enough for the day. Maddy calls Janelle and provides the building management company with her business insurance information. For the first time in a while I have a slight feeling that everything may be OK.

Maddy sits on the couch with earbuds in responding to comments on her social media accounts, previewing the next day's content, and doing whatever else it is that she seems to always be doing on her phone.

"I heard from my old job," I confess to Brian, "it sounds like they're struggling after laying a bunch of people off and have decided that they want to hire some of us back as contractors. I'm not really sure if it's an amazing career move, but it would definitely be a paycheck."

"That's great to hear," Brian says enthusiastically. "You know once ya sorta hit a certain age, I hate to say it, but I feel like opportunities are tougher to come by. Even if it isn't the dream gig, a paycheck is a paycheck and at least you sort of know what you're getting into, right?"

"Yeah," I agree. "I mean part of me wants to tell them to go to hell and watch them struggle to get all their work done without me. But I think that's one of those drinking the poison in hopes that you get to watch someone else suffer sort of situations. Or whatever that metaphor is." Brian smiles and nods along, suddenly seeming a bit shy.

"She seems like a sweet kid," he changes the topic and nods over in Maddy's oblivious direction.

"She is," I agree. "I mean she most certainly tried

with me today." I spin around slowly like I'd done this morning to show off my before and after shots. "I know I am quick to make fun of a lot of the social media stuff that people put up there, but I don't think I realized how much hard work really goes into it until I saw what I saw today. It's really a full-time job for her and all these people that she employs."

"It's impressive, though not sure I can say the same about your makeover results. But it's really.... something," Brian laughs. "Forgot to tell you, I watched one of those 90s movies you recommended. *Singles.*"

"Really?" I reply incredulously. "Aww, I love that movie."

"Ya," he says. "I don't know if totally holds up, but it definitely brought me back. You know the music, the sorta hopefulness of it. The world without phones and all that. Honestly, I think I missed a lot of that in my rush to be a grown up back then, so it was a good little escape. Thanks for the recommendation."

The banter dwindles a bit into semi-silent awkwardness as he gathers the last of his tools that are strewn about and puts them in his bag.

"I should probably go downstairs and see how Marco's doing with the last of the repairs. We need to get the van back to the lot before we clock in too much overtime."

"Absolutely," I acknowledge. "I promised Maddy we'd order take out, so we should probably think about ordering soon. But thank you again for handling all this and taking care of it, I really appreciate it. And hopefully you'll be spared having to see my water disasters for a while."

"Well," he hesitates, "it's not all bad." He looks at me with a bit of a smirk.

"Yeah, but I know it's out of your way and all," I break eye contact slightly uncomfortable. "But thank you for everything, you're a plumbing wizard."

"Right," he says. "No problem, it's the job. Ummm, good luck Jackie and nice to meet you Maddy."

Maddy waves and I close the door behind Brian as he steps out into the hall and proceeds down the stairs. I join her in the living room and flop into a chair.

"Cringe and burn Jackie, geez," she says with disdain. I look at her with confusion.

"Maddy, it's been too long of a day for me to pull out my decoder ring," I reply. "What are you saying?"

"I mean, that guy was totally into you and trying to, you know, ask you out or whatever it is people your age do, and you sorta just blew him off and threw him out," she declares. I immediately scoff, but then start replaying the exchange in my head wondering if I said or did something inappropriate. Had a missed a signal?

"Brian?" I ask half laughing. "He was just being nice to the wacky Little Mermaid lady who's going through a midlife crisis. He's a nice guy and he's paid to be a nice guy by my building." As I say this, I find myself suddenly hoping that maybe Maddy is right and I'm the one misinterpreting the situation.

"Oh-kay," she says. "But that's not what I saw. I think he's into you."

"You think?" I blush, feeling flattered at the prospect that anyone would think of me in a remotely flirty manner. "I kinda thought there might be something there the other day when we had coffee. Then of course I was like, is he really my type? Then I started to beat myself up for even thinking I even had the right to think I have a type." I pause, recognizing that I have suddenly started sharing the hamster-wheel thoughts of my brain out loud.

"A type?" she asks.

"I think I was thinking, at least at first, he might just be a ... dude," I start walking around in a circle making mocking gestures with my hands and body that coincide with the international sign of being a big dumb jock.

"Oooh," Maddy sits up more interested. "I didn't realize you were interested in women, aunt Jack. Is this new or were you always?"

"No," I correct. "It's not that he's male. I think at first, and I'm embarrassed to even say this out loud now that I've gotten to know him a bit, I may have just made a snap first impression about him because he's a big guy with a mustache. I thought he might be one of those big, lumbering, loud Chicago guys who, you know, probably spends the weekends watching sports, mowing his lawn, and grilling meat. You know, like a *dude*, just like plodding through life sorta content to just be, I dunno, ordinary. Like the equivalent of my job at Reed Publishing, just sorta uninventive and 'basic' - something you have to do, but don't want to do. Like a dude's fine to chat with on the bus or at the neighborhood block party, but one day you'll just be sitting on the couch and think, this is what I've chosen for my life?"

"Kinda judgy," aunt Jack, Maddy's face scrunches up.

"I know, and honestly after we started talking and grabbed a coffee, I felt like such an ass for even remotely thinking that he might be like that, because he genuinely seems like a nice guy that gives me a little bit of a flirty butterfly feeling when I talk to him," I sigh.

"So why don't you ask him out?" she asks. "I'll be honest aunt Jack, I mean I love uncle Dan, but he's always been a slightly mopey guy who dresses like he's 15. I don't know if that's a type that's any better than any other guy."

One of the most interesting parts in the aftermath of a divorce is that people feel free to tell you what they've always thought about your former significant other. While many may simply hint at unkind traits to help buoy your spirits, others reveal bigger things like they never liked him or thought that my being with him made me less happy or seemingly depressed. When I first started receiving this kind of feedback, it made me angry in that I often took it as an afront to my own life choices. It was as if them saying bad things about Dan meant they were actually saying bad things about me. However, at this point, with enough time and distance, I can now say that I appreciate any unflattering comments about him as he is no longer my problem or a reflection of me.

"Point taken, Mads," I laugh. "I think my inability to imagine anyone showing interest in me is just a self-esteem problem on my end kiddo. I think the fact that Dan, you know someone I thought I knew so well, left me for another much younger woman, really shook me to my core. And then losing my job on top of all of that, I'm just not sure I trust my inner barometer about much of anything these days. But having a little outside observer, particularly MadLove herself tell me I should go for it, definitely makes me want to give it a bit more thought." I poke her side jokingly and

I pause, "Can I ask you a question, Ms. MadLove?"

"Yeah," she says, "only if you stop calling me that."

"What's up with your love life?" I ask. "I mean, I know I'm just your nosy aunt and probably have no idea what goes on. But I see all these people so excited to see you and everything, everywhere we went today. Does that make it hard to date?"

"People don't like, I dunno, date as much anymore, Jack," she dismisses. "I mean, I've hooked up a few times, but you know it gets weird. Guys can be weird, they think, like everything is a porn movie and every girl wants to be choked or whatever. Dating girls can be just as bad because they can be clingy and think that like, one DM means you're in love with them. If I'm on the apps or whatever I have to be careful that people aren't going out with me just to get more followers or whatever. It gets gross and cringe. It's just kinda not really my priority right now as I build my brand."

I try harder than I did even during the makeover to keep a neutral expression and not react as she speaks, recognizing getting Maddy to open up to me or anyone is probably no small feat. That said, deep down I want to react in horror and protectively shield her when hearing that people have tried to choke her or stalk her as a fucked-up sign of affection.

"Can I give you some advice?" I ask. "And I know I'm probably the last person you think is qualified to give advice, because I know you think you have it all figured out. But, Mads, you're 23. Sweetie, you look better than you'll ever look and you have more opportunities than you'll ever have. If tomorrow you decide you want to be a doctor, a pastry chef, a dog walker, or a professional comedian, there's still time to try to make all those things come true. Experiment, try, and wonder. Sleep with the hot guy, the ugly guy, the funny guy, or, sorry girl, or non-binary person, though never put up with anyone treating you badly. I know people say you can always turn things around or start over, but it really does get harder down the line. Live it up in real life, I'm in awe of all you built with this online world, but I just worry you're missing out in some way."

Maddy sits on the couch quietly and for the first time in a long time she seems to actually be listening to me rather than just picking up her phone and telling me I don't understand.

"I just have to do this for a few more years, Jack," she says steel-faced. "You know, put on the façade and create the illusion of a perfectly curated life even if it's all fake. Once my investments and nest egg are at a level I'm really comfortable with, I can sort of phase out of the hustle and fall back on passive income. Then I can figure out the personal life stuff."

"Mad-dy," I sigh. "It may be too late by then. I mean there will always be a pull to have more money, more stuff, more whatever. Relationships and experiences are what are harder to come by. It must be exhausting to not be sort of living in the real world."

"You don't know the half of it, aunt Jack," she brushes me off. We sit quietly for a moment and I can tell that maybe there is something more she wants to say, but I'm careful not to push too hard.

"Let's get food, ya?" I break the silence.

Our conversation shifts from deep to superficial over Thai food, and by the end of the night I'm glad to say farewell for now, knowing I'll see her Saturday for Cameron's graduation party where I'm sure she'll pick up the never-ending conversation about content views, impressions, sponsorship deals, and collaborations. Hey, I tried.

Exhausted after a day with more physical and emotional activity than I've had in a long time, I go into the bathroom and begin my de-makeover. I look in the mirror and literally burst out laughing. My eyebrows, which have been drawn into an arch about a half inch higher than their actual existence, make me look like Bette Davis in *Whatever Happened to Baby Jane.*

I unclip the hair extensions, wash my face several times over, and take off the ridiculous crop top and high waisted jeans. I slip on a super soft robe that Riff and Arlo left me in the bathroom to replace the ratty robe that I'd had since college which had been hanging on the hook behind the door. I crawl into bed admiring my new accent wall and artwork. My nightstand has a new mid-century inspired lamp sitting on it, and none of the clutter that I normally pile on top. I open the top drawer and find my nightguard and kindle stacked neatly inside, next to a still-in-the package vibrator. I pull it out and read a Post-it note stuck on top, "Even this needed an upgrade. You're welcome – Riff."

I wake up Friday morning and remember the state that my life is actually in. While I'm waiting for my coffee, I decide to accept the contract position. "Fuck it," I mutter. I pick up my phone and call the lawyer. They offer to review the contract for me on my behalf for a small fee, of course, and I tell them I can start in two weeks. Two weeks. This should give me some time to finally enjoy being unemployed knowing that a paid gig is around the corner.

I'm not going to text Liz to let her know just yet, because I'm slightly embarrassed that I've decided to go back. It's like breaking up with someone, bad mouthing them and pointing out their faults, and then having to tell all your friends you're back together weeks later. I'll get in touch, but I just needed a few more days to fully absorb this.

I stand around and marvel at the job Arlo and Riff

did revamping my apartment, minus the hole in the wall, and I notice several new t-shirt dresses tucked into my closet that I hadn't seen earlier. They have Post-it notes on them. "This is what the color black is supposed to look like. Wash in cold. – Riff." The parent I'd never had.

I touch all my books and photo albums now prominently displayed on my back wall as I play some of my record albums that I hadn't been able to find in years because they were buried in boxes in the basement storage area of my old apartment with Dan. I went to school for art history, and most of the books are large format and feature many of my favorite artists from years ago. Much like my early dreams of being somehow ensconced in the museum and gallery world, these books have remained closed and unvisited for decades.

I hesitate before pulling down my wedding album, a small craft-store version of a binder with mismatched sized photos placed in plastic sleeves. We hadn't wanted to spend the money on a photographer, so we had asked friends to send whatever pictures they took to us after the fact to assemble some sort of photographic evidence of our wedding day.

I'm wearing a satin-y knee length slip dress with black Doc Marten boots and a short choppy haircut. I barely recognize myself. I remember arguing with my mother that morning about my dress being inappropriate and I remember my father shaking his head when he saw Dan wearing a t-shirt with holes in it under his suit jacket as he walked me down the aisle. Most of all I see myself as Maddy, a young person thinking she has it all figured out, and is about to go on an adventure, creating a life that everyone will look at in awe.

While musically and artistically I can still relate to that young woman, I realize now that my priorities seem to have changed without my even realizing it. Uncertainty is fun and hopeful when you're 23 and the world is your oyster; less so when you're 52 and legitimately worried whether you'll be able to pay for your rent or ever be able to stop working and retire. The young version of me could think of no bigger failure than becoming a basic sell-out; a mainstream, norm-core person. But as Maddy and her Gen Z counterparts aim to become kings and queens of the sell-outs, I'm starting to realize that fighting to be different or alternative simply for the sake of saying you're different, may not have been the best or happiest life strategy.

That evening, while contemplating many facets of my life, I eat a weed gummy, and reinstall the dating app that I'd deleted in a huff after the terrible date with Javier312. Over the next hour I scroll and swipe looking at the options the algorithm serves me. There were multiple versions of Dan, who come in various colors, sizes, and ages. Men with beanies, thick glasses, and inflated and pretentious answers to their introductory questions. While my eyes gravitate to these options, I find that my slightly high and getting higher heart does not. If the definition of insanity is doing the same thing over and over and expecting a different result, I wonder if choosing to try to date a Dan stand-in would be doing just that.

As I drift off to sleep, Maddy's words about being quick to judge buzz in my head. But before I fully fall asleep, Riff's new and improved "personal massager" buzzes quite effectively much further down my body.

EIGHT

My alarm goes off at 8:30 on Saturday morning. I'd promised Debbie that I'd help her set up for Cameron's graduation party in the backyard. While Debbie's parties are always flawlessly executed, her nervous energy before, during, and after make me wonder if she's ever truly enjoyed one.

I put on one of the new t-shirt dresses that Riff left for me and apply a small amount of the new moisturizer, makeup, and hair products that I'd gotten from the makeover. Despite the attitude at the hair salon and the hideous result with extensions, the actual cut itself was quite cute - a modern shoulder length bob that fell effortlessly to show off my graying stripe in a way that makes it seem intentional rather than unkempt.

I grab the card I'd bought for Cameron, with its cheesy inspirational words on the inside along with a Post-it IOU telling him that I'll give him some money once I start getting paid again. I think back to my own high school graduation and realize that this may be the modern equivalent of an obscure savings bond that my older relatives slipped into cards for me. Busses and trains get me to the suburbs by 10 am where Tom picks me up from the station.

"Hey Jackie," my brother-in-law greets me, "brace yourself for today. Deb is in one of her super intense moods." An NPR story about bees is emanating from the minivan's stereo at a volume more appropriate for someone rocking out to a heavy metal opus.

"Uh oh," I joke. "How many times has she already sent you out for ice and whatever else she claims to have forgotten, even though you know she has it super under control?"

"You don't even know," he laughs. "Poor Cam whispered to me earlier that he wasn't sure he even wanted a party anymore." Tom is a super laid-back guy who would do anything for Debbie and the kids. To me, he was always boring and safe, or as Dan would say "whipped." However, looking at him sitting next to me now, and knowing how he's been patiently sticking by Debbie in a sexless marriage, I wonder if he's more of a devoted hero or on the precipice of having his own mid-life nervous breakdown.

I tell him about the funny portions of spending the

day with Maddy and her team and he shakes his head.

"Sometimes I look at her and Cam and wonder how we created two such different kids," he says. "Maddy somehow has figured out a way to capitalize on just going about her day and sharing what she eats, wears, and sleeps on, and Cameron behaves like he would prefer to live under a rock and never meet another person if he didn't have to. I love them to death, don't get me wrong, but maybe you did the right thing in not having kids, Jack. I feel like half the time I'm worried they're gonna end up alone and then the other half I'm worried that they don't know how to be alone."

I wonder the same thing, but I squeeze Tom's shoulder and try to reassure him that they will definitely find their way in the world. Cameron comes out to the car just as we pull into their driveway.

"Dad, mom is freaking out," he says pleadingly. "She doesn't think there's gonna be enough food. She wants you to go to Jewel and get some more sides, like potato salad and stuff. She also says that grandma is now refusing to come unless someone picks her up at her house. She saw on the news last night someone was stabbed on the train or something so she's saying she won't get stabbed just to come to a graduation party."

"Jesus Christ," I sigh. "Does your grandmother

think someone wants to rob mean little old ladies midday going to the suburbs? I don't know what news she watches, but this is her new panicky thing."

"Hi aunt Jack," Cameron smiles politely looking panicked. While Debbie has the ability to appear calm and composed no matter what's going on in her life, Cameron clearly did not inherit this gene. He looks like a 6-foot-tall string-bean that wants to crawl inside of himself. He's biting his nails and hunching over like a frazzled nervous wreck.

"Hi hon," I smile back. "Here, you get in and take my seat and go with your dad to get the food and deal with grandma. I'll go in and help your mom. Give you two guys a bit of a break."

"Thanks Jackie," Tom sighs.

Cameron gets in the car and I walk up the driveway bracing myself to deal with Debbie in her manic state. I open the door and hear her vacuum going at a high rate of speed. I catch a glimpse of her still wearing her bathrobe with two curlers clipped in at the crown of her hairline.

"Good morning, Mrs. Doubtfire," I joke, preparing to have her throw something at me. "I hear you have everything under control."

"Oh thank God," she says as she turns off the vacuum. "Can you go start cutting up limes for drinks in the kitchen? I'm just gonna finish up here and then go get dressed. Did Cam tell you about mom? She thinks she's gonna get stabbed because someone eight miles away got stabbed on a train at three in the morning. The woman has lived in Chicago all her life and lived through the 1970s for fuck's sake. She really thinks a trip up to the suburbs on a Saturday afternoon is gonna get her killed?"

"Today is not about her Debs, put it out of your mind." She shakes her head and waves her hand in disbelief.

I get out of the line of fire to let her continue vacuuming and take my position in the kitchen as expert lime-cutter. The house looks immaculate, and it smells like some new type of scented candle that I'm sure is appropriately labelled "graduation party." There are "congratulations!" banners hung from the ceiling in the family room and out on the deck where coordinated cups, plates, and napkins are placed at several spots creating food stations. Having just encountered shy and shellshocked Cameron in the driveway, I wonder if he would've preferred that Debbie just Venmo him whatever she spent on the cost of this party as a gift, rather than have to deal with all this fanfare and frenzy.

For the remainder of the morning, Debbie barks orders at me and I dutifully oblige, filling coolers with ice, making pitchers of iced tea and lemonade, filling large bowls with chips and snacks, and then setting up, taking down, and re-setting up folding chairs in various spots on their deck as she contemplates what constitutes the perfect seating arrangement.

By early afternoon, nearly an hour before any guests are slated to arrive, I'm already exhausted and sweaty. Maddy arrives and helps manage her mother by telling her how wonderful everything looks and taking pictures and videos that help boost Debbie's confidence. Fifteen minutes later Tom and Cameron return with grocery bags full of prepared salads and sides that Debbie declares is "all wrong" leaving Tom and Cameron looking dejected.

"Where's mom?" I ask Tom.

"Get this one," he shakes his head, lowering his voice so that Debbie can focus on a potato salad disaster rather than the one he's about to tell me. "We go to the store, get all this stuff, and then go all the way over to her place. Cam rings the bell to go get her and she's wearing pajamas. He waves me over, because I'm double parked sitting out in the car. I go up there and see her and am like, Maggie, what's going on? We have perishables in the car, we gotta go. She said she isn't coming because she's not feeling well and frankly is offended that we didn't offer to pick her up until after she called and told us about the train being unsafe. She said she's not coming where she's not wanted."

"What?" I ask. "I mean she's always been dramatic, but that seems next level even for her."

"I dunno what her deal is," Tom looks over his shoulder. "With Cam looking all forlorn and then having all this food in the car I was like, OK Maggie, suit yourself. And I just walked away."

"You're my hero, Tom," I laugh. "Me and Debbie would've spent 20 minutes arguing with her and still would've ended up with the same outcome. Good for you!"

"This party is for Cam," he says. "If she can't make it not about her for one day, there's no reason to ruin it for everyone else."

"Well done," I wink. "Now we just need to get your wife under control," I joke.

"Yeah, well," Tom starts to speak but thinks twice and cuts himself off. I smile at Tom feeling sorry for what my sister is undoubtedly putting him through because she's afraid to communicate.

"I'll break the news to Debbie about mom, if she even notices," I concede. "You've dealt with enough Novak lady drama for one day. I got you, bud."

"You have no idea," he says. "Thanks Jack."

"Now your only job of the day is to rescue me if you see Dan and his pregnant child bride heading in my direction," I joke. "My mother may be nuts, and your wife may currently be a maniac, but I might not be able to be trusted near the knives with him."

"Dan's having a mid-life crisis of another variety,"

he says. "Except that doofus went off and made his crisis permanent by deciding to have a child in his fifties. Who does that? I barely had energy to have kids when I was in my late twenties. I couldn't possibly imagine having one *now*. He has no idea what he's done."

"If you two could stop chit chatting and help me out, that would be great," Debbie says passive aggressively from across the kitchen. Tom and I give each other knowing looks and proceed to fulfill our assigned tasks.

Tom fills additional coolers that appear out of nowhere with soda and beer, Maddy starts vlogging or doing something phone related, I take the recently acquired groceries and put them in fancier bowls and dishes, and Debbie puts on clothes and make up to promote an illusion that she simply threw a quick party together and hasn't been stressing about it for months. While Maddy has the need to make a world of strangers think her life is perfect, Debbie is the Gen X version where she needs to make sure people she actually knows think that about her. I may have a bit of that, though my goal has always been less about people thinking I'm perfect and more about them thinking I was eccentric, alternative, and interesting. If I stop to think about it, perhaps, we all have been over-curating our life based on what other people might think and would be better served by simply living a life that makes us happy.

Guests start arriving and I'm struck by how few of them are actually young people. I sort of assumed that the majority of the party attendees would be friends of Cameron's from school or the neighborhood, but in fact the bulk are the parents of Cam's schoolmates who Debbie has known over the years from parent groups and activities. The actual classmates are nowhere to be found. At one point, Maddy is holding court for a group of moms talking about her various social media channels. They're hanging on her every word, as if they finally get a seat at the popular girls' high school lunch table. Debbie's standing behind her looking like a dance mom living vicariously through her daughter.

I recognize one of those in the group surrounding Maddy as Anna, Dan's fiancé, who is dressed in a form fitting wrap dress that accentuates her baby bump. Fantastic. She is of course one of those people who remains thin and fit during her pregnancy and just looks like she swallowed a basketball. In fact, I feel like I look more pregnant than she actually does.

"Hey Jack," I swivel around to see Dan standing behind me. "Looks like Debbie's pulled out all the stops as always." It annoys me that he still talks about my sister like he's part of the family.

"Yeah," I agree. "It was mayhem a few hours ago here, but she pulled it off."

"How've you been?" he asks sincerely.

"Good, I got the job thing mostly sorted, so much better now," I gloss over.

"Good for you," he says.

"You?" I ask. "Is your life a baby planning and nesting comedic movie montage right now?"

"Ahhh," he runs his hands through his hair. I realize that it's the first time in ages that I've actually seen his hair in public as it is usually covered by a beanie. Thinning at the top and much grayer than it was just a few months ago, he looks less man-child than usual. "If I'm being honest, it's been a lot. Like marriage, baby, a new relationship, moving, the divorce. There're definitely days when I feel like I've bit off way more than I can chew. Anna's great, but she's just …" He drops his voice to just above a whisper. "… you know, younger and comes at things with a whole different perspective."

"Yup," I say. I hope that my closed lip expression is passive aggressive enough to convey an underpinning of both "told you so" and "serves you right."

"Guess I deserve that," he responds. My shorthand message is thankfully not lost on him.

"You'll figure it out," I say half compassionately half condescendingly. "I mean you kinda just have to."

"I know," he agrees. He swirls his beer around in his glass. "I miss you, Jack. Not in like in a wife way, but like in a friend way." I scrunch my face not sure if I should be offended or flattered.

"Well, I hope we can get to that point again," I say not quite sure if I mean it. I look over at Anna who's been side eyeing us from the Maddy gossip circle. "But I don't think it's gonna be today. I wish you the best, I really do, but I just need time. You broke my heart, and upended my life. Maybe at some point I'll see this as a good thing, but I'm still picking up the pieces." I don't know why I feel the need to confess this to him. I had plenty of time to pour my heart out during the divorce discussions, but I was so hurt and defensive that I put up a ten-foot wall and stopped sharing anything vulnerable with him. Seeing him here, now, with his pregnant fiancée, in a way, gives me closure and perhaps a window to share a glimpse of honesty.

"I'm sorry, Jack," he says sincerely. "I really am."

He steps away to join his soon-to-be wife and I look over at him through a different lens. I see a scared man who's attempting to reclaim his youth by marrying someone far too young and making different decisions this time around. True, I may have extended my youth for a little too long, but I finally feel that I'm moving in the right direction and becoming the adult I need to be.

I look around and realize that I don't see Cameron

anywhere. It's nearly 7 pm and I wonder if he had the urge to sneak out just as much as I do now. I go inside and walk upstairs where I find Cam sitting on his bed reading a book.

"Hey, kiddo," I say. "Everything OK?"

"Yeah," he replies. "I'm just sorta done with all that party stuff. It's all mom's friends anyway."

I look around his room which still has the wallpaper, bedding, and some of the posters on the wall that he had since he was ten years-old and Debbie redid his room. I think back to my own teenage bedroom and remember it being papered with *Rolling Stone* and *SPIN* magazine covers of my favorite bands, movie posters, and smelling like incense sticks that I bought from hippie stores that I thought were so cool to burn to cover up the cigarette smoke smell on my clothes. It's as if Cameron chose not to partake in being a teenager and still lives as a young child with a life curated by his mother.

"Yeah, I get it," I agree. "So what's next for you, Mr. High School graduate? Any idea? And there is no wrong answer, because frankly if you ask me what's next I would have no clue either." He looks at me slightly pleased that someone is actually talking to him and asking him questions rather than just telling him what to do.

"I think I'm going to become a game developer," he says matter-of-factly.

"Seriously?" I reply taken aback. "I didn't know that was something you could do or were into."

"I mean," he starts. "I'm self-taught and all, but I'm hoping to get a job at one of the smaller companies and then sorta learn on the go from there." I look around again wondering if I missed seeing a giant gaming chair or the hallmark computer paraphernalia that one stereotypically associates with a gamer kid. There is nothing in sight. Does he know that one actually has to play and create games to be a game developer? Or is this part of his world so underground that it's right in front of my eyes, but I can't see it?

"Really? I mean your mom never mentioned any of this. I honestly had no idea."

"Yeah, well," he says, "I think Maddy takes up a lot of her time and attention. But I've kinda got a following online and already have some interest from some west coast companies, so I think by the end of the summer something should come through."

I smile at him, now prouder of my weird nephew than I'd ever been. While his sister has been out broadcasting every meal, sneeze, and thought, he was inside quietly building an empire doing what he loved.

"That's amazing, Cam," I say sincerely.

"Thanks, aunt Jackie," he smiles appreciatively. We sit in his room quietly for a few more minutes and

I appreciate the ease with which we can just hang out and in his case, not say anything.

"Can you do me a favor?" I ask, breaking the silence. "Can you sneak out with me and drive me to the station? I have a few things to do tonight and I want slip out without your mom giving me more jobs."

"Sure, aunt Jack," he agrees. "No one seems to miss me anyway."

"I see you Cam," I say out of nowhere. "And you are gonna be just fine."

He smiles awkwardly at me having no idea what the hell I'm talking about, but appreciating that someone cares. I realize that those exact words are what I really need someone to say to me right about now, but it makes me happy that I can pay it forward and give him the boost that he needs. We go out of the front of the house, with everyone still in the backyard and he drives me to the station. I hug him and walk up to the platform realizing that at some point Debbie will realize I left, but hopefully it will be after she's had several hard seltzers to soften the blow.

Google maps tells me a train, a bus, and another train will land me at either my best or worst idea of the evening in about an hour. While on the train I apply some travel deodorant, fluff my hair, and apply a new coat of lipstick like a teenager taking the bus to high school. My stomach feels unsettled which I hope is just nerves and not reflective of the Jewel Osco potato salad Tom picked up.

I arrive at 8:30 pm and stand across the street wondering if I'm actually going to do what I'm about to do. I watch as a few people stand outside to smoke and chat. Once they go inside, I decide to make my move. From the outside, O'Brien's is one of those classic far Northwest side Chicago bars with glass blocks in place of traditional windows making it nearly impossible to see inside and what you are about to walk into.

I open the door to the bar revealing a larger space than I expected. At the front is a wall mounted jukebox and some small two-top tables, additional tables line the left wall, and a long bar extends to the back opening up to another room. The place is fairly busy for a Saturday night, so thankfully the loud conversations and music mask my entrance and only a few curious heads sitting at the end of the bar turn around when I walk in. I smile and pretend I'm looking for a friend, which, in theory, I am.

After a moment or two of feeling like an idiot for assuming Brian would be here, I spot him at the other end of the bar sitting next to a blonde middle-aged woman laughing with beers in front of them. It occurs to me that I never asked him if he was currently dating anyone or in a relationship of any kind. I'd made this bold move based on the gut feeling of a 23-year-old who has never dated anyone and the fact that a plumber who's paid to provide good customer service was kind to me. My brain starts to explode with embarrassment as I realize I have taken two trains and a bus over an hour to surprise a guy who was just being nice because he's a competent employee. Fuck.

I turn around to leave before he sees me.

"Jackie?" I hear behind me in a booming voice. "JACKIE!?" the voice summons. I turn around to see Brian standing up next to his seat with his hands in the air in a what-are-you-doing-here fashion. The whole bar is now looking in my general direction and I give them all a sheepish wave. I take the longest walk I've ever taken toward the back of the bar and approach Brian and the woman he's sitting with.

"Hey," I say trying to drown out the sound of my own heartbeat in my ears. He looks at me quizzically. I honestly am not sure what to say. The only thing that comes to mind, thanks to the movie *Singles* which has been on a loop in my head for 30-plus years, is "I was...just nowhere near your neighborhood." His quizzical smile turns into a large grin that soothes my need to throw up.

"What took you so long," he replies, having just watched the movie himself. His response mimics the dialogue of the movie's main characters reuniting after a bout of insecurity. I hadn't just made a fool out of myself with this giant leap of faith that might also qualify as light stalking. "Jackie, this is my sister-in-law Caroline," he gestures toward the blonde woman he's been talking to. "She's my brother Chris's wife. Chris is behind the bar and will gladly get you a drink if you'd like."

"Yes please," I say with relief on all counts.

"Nice to meet you hon," Caroline smiles. "I'll let you take my seat, I gotta get home and walk the dogs anyway. I just like to drop by and give the guys a bit of a hard time."

"Great meeting you," I wink. She touches my arm and hugs Brian goodbye. I take her seat, order a pint of Guinness, and for the first time since I arrived sit and make full on eye contact with Brian.

"You look a little different than the last time I saw you," he jokes. "I almost didn't recognize you without all the makeup and hair."

"Can you believe that?" I say with ease. He's turned his barstool to face me and his long legs are on either side of mine. As my heart rate finally starts to slow down, I'm able to take him in. He's wearing a t-shirt with the Chicago Bears logo on it except is says BEERS. His mustache is more manicured than when I saw it the other day and he smells like you would hope someone in a soap commercial would smell like. Chris puts the pint down in front of me and I catch a glimpse of a cheeky knowing look exchanged between brothers.

"Soooo," Brian starts. "Welcome to my home away from home. Well, actually, it pretty much was our home growing up. I live a few blocks from here now so, I guess I should just say welcome to my world."

"I like it," I awkwardly look around feeling like a teenager who just passed a note to a boy she likes in her third period English class. I take a gulp of my beer.

"I'm glad you're here Jackie," he leans in and touches my leg. "I'm a little shocked, but very pleasantly surprised."

"I ummm," I stammer. "This is probably the boldest move I've ever made, if I'm being honest. But I kinda felt there might be something there. Maddy saw it too and kinda gave me a little push. And other than flooding my apartment again, which I'm sure can be arranged, I wasn't sure how else I'd get to meet up with you. I remembered you said you hang out here on weekends, so I decided to give it a shot. Plus, I had to hang out with my sister who was losing her mind all day with my nephew's high school graduation party, so I really needed a drink."

"Well, it's great seeing you out in the real world," he winks. "I went to Maddy's YouTube and

Instagram and stuff and liked and subscribed like I was supposed to."

"That's so sweet," I say taken aback.

"I'll be honest, I have no idea what the fuck she's talking about or why so many people seem to be so interested in everything she's saying, but ya know, I'm happy to support the kid."

We spend the next few hours talking and laughing and easing into a rhythm of witty banter like we've known each other for years. With each new pint of beer our conversation involves more innocent touching and hands resting on each other's limbs. I learn more about his daughters, his childhood, embarrassing moments, and favorite things. I tell him about my dramatic mother, my hatred of karaoke, how I could happily eat Stan's donuts for every meal if it wouldn't kill me, and how I'm trying to figure out some new hobbies given my new life situation.

"You might find this hard to believe," he confesses, "but I'm somewhat of an expert gardener."

"What?" I cock my head.

"Ya, when I bought my house years ago, the old woman who owned it for like decades was going into a nursing home. She'd turned the backyard into this massive garden of flowers and vegetables, some raised beds and such. It had sorta gotten all overgrown because she couldn't really take care of it well anymore, but she took me around and told me what everything was. So I kinda got really into it. So much of my day job is spent inside, in people's basements or under porches or whatever. It's just nice and relaxing to spend time outside making things grow. I don't even mind weeding and stuff. And you know being 6'4" who the fuck is gonna give me shit about liking to garden," he laughs.

"That's amazing," I say sincerely.

"Ya, I really got into it, reading books, joining the local seed club, the whole deal. And as you would expect, my irrigation system is top notch!" He excuses himself to go to the bathroom and I take a moment to finally look up and see that many of the patrons in the bar are stealing looks in my direction likely sizing up the new girl talking to their hometown boy.

I resist the urge to pull my phone out and text Debbie as I feel the need to stay present. Instead, I continue to look around and take in my environment and the characters surrounding me.

"Hey red," an older man sitting midway down the bar says in my direction. "You Irish?" The cadre of regulars sitting around him all swivel around to hear the answer and take stock of the newbie at their bar.

"Close," I say. "Polish. So we're basically related by blood through the potato," I wink. The guys start laughing, satisfied that I have a sense of humor and am able to quickly respond to their banter.

"You giving her a hard time, Pat?" Brian jokes as he returns to his stool. Pat waves him off and turns back to his friend to nurse his beer.

"This place," he jokes. "You lose track of time when you're here. Ole Pat over there has been on that stool for like 40 years. Though speaking of which, I checked my watch when I was in the bathroom and didn't realize how late it is. I guess time flies in good company." I look at my watch and see that it's nearly midnight.

"Wow is right," I agree. "You don't have to work tomorrow, do you?"

"No," he dismisses. "We rotate being on call on the weekends, and I'm not up until the end of the month."

We sit in anticipatory silence for what feels like an eternity, but is only a few moments, neither one of us exactly sure what comes next. Our legs are now somewhat intertwined with one of his resting on the outside of mine and the other between them, a common configuration for Dan and I for the bulk of our barstool days.

"I'm sure you probably want to get home," he starts, "or, you know, have something to do in the morning. But if you have a little time, I just live a few blocks from here and can show you my garden if you're interested."

"I would love to see your garden…in the dark," I smirk and shake my head up and down slowly. I'm relieved that he seems to have made the next move because after the major risk I took in just showing up here I'm not sure I'm capable of executing another big move tonight.

"Fantastic," he smiles. "I do my best gardening in the dark."

We get up and he puts his hand on my back as I make my way around the bar. He shakes the hands of nearly everyone sitting around still enjoying their pints and waves to his brother. They all smile at me likely wondering if they will ever see me again, as I wonder the same thing.

We walk the few blocks to his house arm in arm as he gives me gossip about the various people who live in the neighborhood pointing out houses along the way. He confesses that one of the fun parts of being a plumber is getting to peek into so many people's lives and living environments. He equates it with being a doctor. Sometimes, you skip all the introductory pleasantries and immediately learn everyone's dirty little secrets hanging out in their bathrooms, closets, and deepest darkest places.

"You'd really be surprised at how many people are secretly hoarders," he says. "Sometimes it's obvious when you pull up and see a yard full of crap. But sometimes its these nice normal looking people who come out and then you go inside and have to walk through these tiny little pathways of junk to get to a kitchen sink that they haven't been able to use in ten years."

"Better you than me," I say with a horrified look. "Though hopefully this isn't your way of telling me that you're secretly a hoarder?" I laugh.

"Guess you're about to find out," he laughs. "This is me." We stand in front of a small Chicago 1950s brick ranch house that looks similar to nearly every other house on the block. "I bought it after my second divorce. Wanted to be close to the kids and my family, but didn't need that much space. So it's been sorta perfect." The lawn and front landscaping are impeccable.

"It's adorable," I add. "You even sculpt topiary bushes?" I point out the pom-pom shaped bushes on either side of his front stairs.

"Oh yeah," he says, "I really know my way around a bush." He raises his eyebrow devilishly, sticks out his tongue, and smiles.

I step up on his front step so that I am nearly eye level with him, put my hands on his face and kiss him slowly and passionately, releasing all the tension that has been building up the whole night. He puts his hands around my waist, making me feel small and protected and kisses me back intentionally as his hand moves up my back.

"Want to move inside before your neighbors start writing into your alderman or the Nextdoor app about their neighbor making out in public?" I laugh.

"Half of them can't see well enough to drive at night," he attempts to whisper as he grabs his keys with his hand still around my waist. "I'm not too worried." We step into his living room and my eyes adjust as he turns on the light.

"My grandparents lived in a ranch just like this in Skokie when I was growing up," I say looking around. "Similar layout." He'd clearly made upgrades over the years as I note the modern touches and lighting. The furniture is contemporary, but classic, avoiding the big leather couches and TV trays that so many middle-aged bachelors mistake as decorating.

"Come on in," he gestures. "I'll give you a quick tour. You want a glass of water?" I nod and we move through the house. "I still have the original pink bathroom," he points out.

"Wow," I say in disbelief. "You're a plumber, I thought you would have some modern shower with like 15 water sprays or something."

"Like I always say, they don't build them like they used to," he throws up his hands. "That bathroom is solid and functional and kinda kitschy. I'm not getting rid of that unless I have to." Something about this big burly guy defending a 1950s pink bathroom tickled me and I stepped in closer to him and we start to kiss again.

"Can I see your bedroom?" I half whisper in a

wanting but embarrassed way.

He takes my hand and leads me into a small bedroom that fits little more than a king-sized bed and a nightstand. Rather than turning on the overhead light, he turns on a dim tableside lamp that casts a warm glow throughout the room. The walls have several framed landscape paintings on them.

"I paint too, sometimes," he sits on the bed and points to the framed art on the walls. My eyes widen into a smile.

"You are a man of many surprises and talents," I run my hand over his beard playfully.

"I'd love to show you some of my other talents, if that's OK," he says quietly as he puts his hands up underneath my t-shirt dress. I nod in agreement as he lifts it up and off over my head.

"You may want to dim the lights a little more," I say self-deprecatingly with a giggle.

"You're beautiful," he stares into my eyes earnestly while running his hands up my back. "Jackie, I mean that." I squirm a bit realizing I'm struggling to take the compliment as it feels genuine versus the creepy lines Javier312 tried to feed me.

"Just so you know, it's been more than a minute since I've been with anyone other than my ex," I confess. "I don't know what the modern making out protocol is. My niece says guys choke people now and do all sorts of weird shit. I'm a little bit more old school about things. I'm probably hairier and heavier than your average porn star. I just want to have fun and feel good. I don't...." I have verbal diarrhea that threatens to put an end to the romantic moment, but I can't quiet the need to tell this man all my sexual insecurities.

"Jackie, I'm a 54-year-old twice divorced plumber," he smiles. "I know how to make sure everyone's pipes are safe and humming smoothly, and you know I prefer vintage pipes, if you know what I mean. That drawer over there isn't just filled with gardening books. I got condoms and lube and probably some other stuff too. If I start to do anything you don't like or want, tell me, and if I don't do something you like or want, tell me. OK?" He holds onto me in an assuring way. "I can't risk getting a bad Yelp review, so you're always in charge." He kisses my cleavage and I'm both stunned and turned on by his sweet directness. I laugh and climb on top of him.

Over the next hour, all the unpleasant memories of the last few weeks, Dan, and my insecurities are erased. Brian explores every nook and cranny of my body with his fingers, tongue and lower half of his body making note of what I need more of and when to keep moving. I fear my skills pale in comparison, but his exploration inspires adventurousness in me and I too become an explorer releasing moans and pleasant groans with each new spot I touch.

As a larger guy, I am amazed with how lightly and gingerly he's able to move on and around me. Much like the other preconceived notions I had about him, he dismantles my assumption that sex with him might feel like being smothered by the lead apron the dentist puts on you when doing X-rays. Instead, I feel safe, seen, heard, and extremely aroused.

I open his nightstand and gesture for him to get a condom. He grabs one, slips it on and then rubs lube on it and into me. I straddle him and he pushes inside of me. With me setting the pace and motion, within moments I'm releasing noises that I don't think have ever escaped before as I orgasm without self-consciousness. Once I reinhabit my body and look at him, he smirks and flips me onto my back despite my being Amazonian in stature with a few extra pounds. Half kneeling half standing he kisses my neck as he grinds between my legs so as not to crush me with the full weight of his body. He finishes with a tightening and release.

"Holy shit," I laugh when I see he has come back into his body. We both start laughing as he extricates himself from inside of me. "You are totally getting a good Yelp review." He kisses me and then goes off to the bathroom to remove the condom, thankfully closing the door behind him so I don't have to watch. Dan had always been the kind of guy who did absolutely everything with the bathroom door open. While I'd made jokes over the years about craving privacy, I never said anything directly about preferring to have some mysteries kept behind closed doors.

When he comes out, I go into the bathroom to pee and take a look at myself and my surroundings. His bathroom is immaculately clean. I look at my tussled hair and sagging breasts in the bathroom mirror and let out a little smirk. I truly feel good.

I walk back into the bedroom and climb under the covers with him, resting my head in the nook of his arm as he rubs my back with a smile on his face. We say very little as we cuddle and drift in and out of consciousness.

The next morning, I wake up to the smell of coffee alone in Brian's large bed. I haven't slept this well in years, particularly without the help of a weed gummy, so part of me is reluctant to move a muscle and have this comfort end. I hunt through the covers and the area surrounding the bed for my bra, underwear, and dress. I run my fingers through my hair and creep into the bathroom to rinse my mouth out with water before having a morning conversation.

I walk into the kitchen and see the back of Brian's head out the kitchen window sitting on his deck. I open the door to join him, noting that the kitchen clock shows it's nearly 10 am.

"Good morning," I smile. "I'm so sorry I slept so late. I hope you didn't have something to do this morning that I held you back from. You could've woken me." He smiles and sticks his arm out to take my hand to lead me to sit beside him on the outside sofa.

"There's coffee inside if you want some. I can get some breakfast going if you want, but I wasn't sure if you had preferences or restrictions. My daughters are always coming home with new ways of eating, so before I offend or accidentally kill you with eggs or toast or something, I thought I'd ask." He's wearing reading glasses and had been scrolling on his phone. I look out into his small, fenced, backyard, and am taken aback by the scope of his gardening.

"You weren't kidding about the gardening," I say sincerely. "This is incredible." There are patches of flowers, raised vegetable beds, herbs, flowering bushes, and tropical plants that I had no idea even grew in Chicago. "It's like you have your own botanical garden back here."

"It's my happy little secret," he smiles. "So ya, breakfast. What can I get you?"

"Are you sure?" I ask. "I don't want to put you out. I know you weren't expecting to have company."

"Jackie, this is the nicest surprise I've ever had,"

he touches my shoulder. "Goat cheese and herb omelet with some sourdough toast, OK?"

"Are you kidding me?" I laugh. "I think you belong in my neighborhood more than I do, making artisan meals with food that you grow and then painting landscapes. I mean…"

"What can I say," he literally pats himself on his back, "I'm a multifaceted modern man! Well, that, and I spent a lot of time in the kitchen growing up. I don't know if you noticed at the bar last night, but that back room, where Chris hosts trivia nights and private parties and stuff now, back when I was a kid, that was a restaurant. My mom used to cook and I spent a lot of time after school and on weekends and stuff helping her back there."

"Sounds like you put your youth to use much more than I did," I raise my hands.

"Well, I wasn't an altar boy," he laughs. "Actually, I literally was an altar boy for a couple of years, but not a good one." He gets up to go in the kitchen. "If you want to grab a shower while I'm cooking, please feel free. I can get you a towel and I actually have a ton of those free toothbrushes the dentist gives you, if you want one of those."

"That would be amazing," I say with relief. "I spent most of the day at the beck and call of Debbie, running around her house organizing stuff and feel like I probably still smell like potato salad and giardiniera."

"No problem. And you don't," he winks. He hands me a bath towel and toothbrush and I take a short but much needed shower in his retro bathroom that has the strongest water pressure that I've experienced in years. When I get out, I smell like his soap and shampoo and wrap the towel around me for a moment breathing it in. I brush my teeth and put on the travel deodorant I have in my purse along with some fresh lipstick. While my crumpled clothes still give off a walk of shame vibe, I am feeling more like a human being.

"Your water pressure is impressive," I say as I touch his back and walk around him to grab another cup of coffee.

"Told you," he says proudly. "If it ain't broke don't fix it." He finishes flipping the omelet and suggests we go eat outside. Between bites, he points to various things in the garden explaining vegetables and flowers that I had only heard of and wouldn't have been able to identify in a supermarket lineup.

We finish up and sit outside chit chatting for a bit, like people who have known each other far longer than we actually have. When the conversation dies down, I look down at my watch and realize it's nearly one in the afternoon.

"I should probably get going," I sigh, worried that I may be overstaying my welcome.

"If you give me 15 minutes to take a quick shower," he says, "I can drive you."

"You don't have to do that," I insist. "You're walkable to the L, I can just grab the Blue Line."

"Jackie," he shakes his head sensing I'm trying to make sure I'm not offending him, "if you are done with me for the day and want to grab the L, be my guest. But I'm enjoying spending time with you and have nothing else to do today. If you weren't here, I'd probably weed some plants and then go harass my brother at the bar. It's far more fun to harass you. I mean it."

"Well, when you put it that way," I smile. "Go shower. We can grab another coffee down by me if you want."

"I want," he agrees. He walks past me and pats my ass as he goes into the bathroom. "Make yourself at home, feel free to put the TV on or whatever. Remote is on the coffee table."

I sit in the living room and pull out my phone, which I've neglected since I entered the bar last night. I have three missed calls and six texts from Debbie.

> Sister Debbie: You left without saying goodbye? WTF JACK? Cam said he drove you to the train. All OK? Love you.

> Sister Debbie: Seriously, Jack. You OK? Are you home?

> Sister Debbie: Where did you go? Jack,

> you're scaring me. Call me.

> Sister Debbie: If this is some kind of punishment for inviting Dan to the party, I'm sorry. But call me back.

Sister Debbie: JACKIE!!!! CALL ME!!

> Sister Debbie: ARE YOU ALIVE?!! WHERE ARE YOU?! TEXT ME BACK OR I'M CALLING THE POLICE OR WORSE, MOM.

Oh geez, that's all I need, having to explain to the cops, or worse, my mother that I wasn't stabbed on the L but instead snuck off from my nephew's high school graduation party to go seduce my plumber.

> Me: I'm alive I'm alive!! Calm down!!! I'm on the NW side. Had a lovely sleepover with my plumber. Ask Maddy about him :) I'll call you tonight when I'm home. Phone is low on charge so may not text back. Don't freak out and for fuck's sake don't call MOM!

Within five seconds my phone buzzes as Debbie begins reacting to my message with the exploding head emoji, followed by every GIF that involves surprise, sex, and plumbers. I chuckle and silence my phone.

"What's so funny?" Brian asks standing in the bathroom doorway wearing only his boxer shorts.

"My sister thought I got murdered last night because I snuck out of her son's graduation party without telling her," I confess. "I alluded to what I got up to so she didn't call the police."

"Ahhhh," he says. "That's actually sweet that she checks up on you. You'd be surprised at how many people don't have that in their life. I think I'm up to about six dead bodies in my career."

"Wait, what?" I ask confused.

"Yeah, we get called in all the time for leaks happening from an upper apartment or some sort of water situation, or someone thinks they smell gas at a neighbor's house. We get an emergency service call and it turns out someone's died and we're the first to find them with like apartment management or someone who has a key or whatever."

"Wow," I shake my head. "You're definitely full of interesting stories Brian O'Brien," I joke. I'm now standing next to him and he smells clean and fresh. I trace the tattoo on his upper arm with my finger, not quite sure what it is because it's faded and spread into a navy-blue blob like so many old tattoos do.

"Don't even ask," he anticipates. "My brothers and I got the same tattoo of the bar's logo when we were teenagers at some half assed place where broke kids got tattoos from people who had no business giving tattoos. Years later my Celtic knot looks more like an ink splotch." I kiss it and then him and then we make out for a few more minutes before I put a stop to it.

"Let's get going, otherwise we're gonna spend the whole day in bed," I declare, still shocked by what this day has turned into.

"And what's wrong with that?" he asks.

"We can try my bed out," I say coyly. He smiles and gets dressed.

He parks near my building and as we walk the two blocks over to the coffee shop, holding hands, we encounter Freddy.

"OH snap!!" he yells laughing in an exaggerated manner. "It's LumberJack-AY! The power couple du jour!"

"Freddy," I sigh.

"You know I'm just kidding with you mama," he laughs again. "What's up big man? Good to see you again."

"You too," Brian smiles.

"Jack-ay, just letting you know I'm gonna be gone for the summer," Freddy says as if he's my assistant or building manager or something. "I'm heading down to Flor-I-DUH for the summer to hang with my daughter."

"I don't think I even knew you had a daughter, Freddy," I reply.

"Ya, she moved down there with her mom years ago, but has her own place now and says she wants to see me and is sending a ticket," he explains.

"That's great Freddy," I say earnestly. The thought that Freddy has a family that cares about him and wants to see him makes me happy. Over the years I've gotten bits and pieces of his life story, but filled in the blanks with bleak assumptions. Hearing that those assumptions might have been wrong is a pleasant surprise. "Behave yourself when you're down there, OK?"

"Girl, have you seen the women down in Florida?" he asks. "You know what I'm talking about Lumberjack? Little skimpy bathing suits and all that!! I'll try to behave, but who knows I may have another daughter down in Florida by the time I leave, if you know what I mean," he laughs again maniacally.

"OK, OK," I say. "Well have a great trip and I'll see you when you're back."

"Yeah mama, thanks," he says. "And you two have a good summer too. When I come back maybe you'll have some lumberjack babies roaming around the hood. Jack-ay still has some life in her left I'm sure," he laughs again and hits me in the arm.

"Good BYE Freddy," I say annoyed. Freddy turns the corner and walks down the street loudly saying hello and making comments to acquaintances and unsuspecting strangers alike along the way.

"A whole summer without Freddy, how will I possibly go on," I laugh as Brian and I continue walking.

"I think it's sweet that you're friendly with him," he acknowledges. "So many people would write him off. I know he's probably a pain in the ass, but even a pain in the ass person deserves kindness."

"If I'm being truthful," I confess, "On a deeper level I probably have always related more to people who are different, down on their luck, or off the beaten path, like Freddy, than even someone like my sister Debbie. You know, like I've always sort of viewed myself as not completely fitting in, sometimes a little too loud or awkward or inappropriate, and just feeling judged as sort of the underdog in every situation. So, while my circumstances may not have me hustling under the L, I think I understand how that could happen, maybe even more so than how someone can have their shit so together." He rubs my shoulders as we walk.

When we ultimately head back to my apartment, Brian roams around looking at everything on my bookshelves and through my vinyl records and shelf of CDs pointing out things that he knows, has, likes, or hasn't heard in years. We take turns in selecting the music to play, each recounting stories of when we first heard it, the memories that it brings back, and Googling "where is the musician now."

"You have so many art books," he comments, thumbing through various titles and pulling some books off the shelves to flip through.

"Yeah, my degree is actually in art history, believe it or not," I confess. "I did some drawing and a bit of painting when I was younger, but I think I always knew I was better at appreciating art than creating it."

"Did you ever try to do anything with it, like in galleries and stuff?" he asks.

"I think back in the day I always sort of felt at home in museums. When I was a kid, my mom would be having one of her sort of explosive episodes yelling at everyone and my dad's solution was to take me and Debbie out to a museum for the day. It would get us out of the house and would give my mom time to calm down from whatever was bothering her that day," I explain. "We went to all sorts of museums and just would roam around, look at art and objects and whatnot, and spend time alone with my dad. So I think I really associate museums and art with like being safe and secure with him."

Brian smiles, listening to everything I say. His attention makes me feel like what I'm saying is actually interesting. Something I haven't felt in a while. Typically, I feel like I am just talking until the person across from me feels comfortable enough to pick up their cell phone to begin scrolling.

"But I guess to answer your question," I continue, "not really. I mean after college I applied to some gallery jobs and art-related positions, but nothing much came of them. The pay for museum work now is pitiful so back then it was even worse. I had college loans to repay and couldn't afford to move out of my parents' place and pay those back on an entry level art-job salary. So basically, I worked everywhere else I could to make ends meet. Ultimately, I got into editing, thinking that maybe one day I could edit art books or something like that, but life happens and that dream died a bit," I laugh half-heartedly.

"It's never too late," Brian reminds me.

I shrug and settle in closer to him, hoping to shift the topic. Snuggling on the couch eventually turns into making out and another incredible round of sex in which he willingly incorporates the new vibrator Riff got me into the mix. I'm shocked by how easily I'm able to verbalize what I want or want to try with him without getting tongue tied or embarrassed. While sex with Dan was always good, at some point the act itself became the equivalent of putting in an express reorder on a take-out food ordering app. Neither one of us ever gave much thought to it and eventually our repertoire became the sex version of our Friday night order of Greek salad, margarita pizza, and two diet cokes. Sex with Brian is like being at a whole new restaurant with cuisine that sounds somewhat familiar but is seasoned, plated, and presented in entirely new and exotic ways.

"I should get going," Brian says grimacing as he looks at the clock and rolls over. "I have an early start tomorrow."

"Can I," I hesitate, "maybe get your number or something so I don't have to flood my apartment or show up at your house unannounced to get in touch?"

"Holy shit," he laughs. "I forgot we never even exchanged numbers." We take each other's phones and enter our information.

"So how does this work," I ask reluctantly. "Do I need to wait two days to text or call or e-mail or whatnot so I seem interested but not needy? I'm a little outta practice."

"I think the way it works now is that you send me nude photos, I send you fruit emojis and whoever accidentally sends the other's photos to a family group text first, wins," he says in a 1980s valley girl voice.

"Oh," I laugh "that will totally be me."

"How about we just go ahead and make a plan to hang out again?" he says confidently. "The only caveat is I head up to northern Wisconsin on

Wednesday night with my daughters. It's sort of a family start-of-the-summer tradition. My brother owns a cabin. Well, he calls it a cabin, but it's a proper house that just doesn't have much in the way of Wi-fi. We all go up there for a long weekend with the kids. I call them kids, but they're in their 20s and 30s at this point. Everyone has a long-term partner of their own, so it can feel quite cramped!"

"Aww," I say, "that sounds lovely. A little off grid time with the family."

"Yeah, it's a good tradition and nice to get out of town for a few days. But all of that is to say, I'll be out of pocket until Sunday afternoon. Once I'm back in a place with service and heading home I can text you and we can figure out what might work depending on traffic and such," he winks.

"Deal," I smile. He leans down and kisses me goodbye. Despite this being pretty much the equivalent of a first date, albeit a very long one, I'm shocked by how familiar and comfortable we are with each other already.

I watch him walk to the end of the hall and I wave as he goes into the elevator. When I hear the doors close, I softly pad to the front window and peek out the curtains to see him disappear toward his car. I flop on the couch, exhausted, and stunned by the outcome of my very out of character and bold move. Looking around the apartment I marvel at how much has changed in the span of a week. My job situation has gone from nothing to sorta, kinda something; I've had sex with a man who seems sensitive and decent; my apartment is clean; and I now have a closet drawer full of fake clip-in hair. I plug my nearly dead phone in and immediately text Debbie.

> Me: Coffee tomorrow morning, my place 9ish? So much to tell.

> Sister Debbie: Yes, slut. Just kidding – JEALOUS!!! Love you.

NINE

I hear my front door open at 8:30 Monday morning and panic. I immediately wonder if I forgot that the building management was coming to fix the wall.

"Hello? It's your favorite sister..." Debbie says in a high-pitched fake British accent. Debbie is one of those people who always travels with an enormous purse and random tote bags full of food, clothing, and essentials that you never knew you needed that makes you wonder if she's staying for 10 minutes or 10 months.

"Why are you so early? And why did I give you a key?" I mumble from bed.

"So I could check on your dead body if I don't hear from you in a few days," she says opening the blinds like our mother used to do when we were kids and didn't want to get up for school. "You're gonna have a job again soon, maybe you need to practice getting up at normal people times."

"Maybe you can give me a day to bask in the latest developments of my life," I counter. "It's taken me years to destroy my life, but apparently I'm able to put it back together in like a week."

"That pretty much sums you up, Jack," she laughs. "Procrastinator puts off getting shit together and then does it in a weekend. Lucky, bitch. What the fuck, tell me everything."

I make us coffee and we sit on the couch as a grin emerges on my face and I try to figure out where to start.

"So did Maddy tell you about the plumber?" I ask. "His name is Brian, by the way."

"Yeah, but she said she wasn't sure you were into him." She pulls out a pair of slippers to put on from one of her bags as well as a bottle of hand lotion that she passes to me, as if she was a psychic dermatologist who anticipated I needed to add moisture to my skin.

"I wasn't really sure and was really just not super confident that anyone could find me all that interesting or attractive in my current state," I confess. "But to her credit, Maddy really gave me the push I needed to try to see things from a different angle and see the possibility in things. So yeah, I mulled it over and then at Cam's party, I saw Dan and what a tool he was being when he realized things were getting real. And I'm like, I've been with my 'type' for like half my life and it ultimately sucked. What's the harm in trying something new?"

"Oh my God," she says. "Not to interrupt, but after you left the party, Dan and Anna were having some sort of argument. I think there's trouble in paradise there. Dan was ready to leave the party and Anna just kept glomming onto Maddy like some sort of pregnant fame whore. They were bickering and all sorts of stuff."

"I got that sense from him too. I also had a really good chat with Tom about Dan and it was just nice to hear his opinion too," I admit.

"What did Tom say?"

"He basically just said that Dan's midlife crisis would now be a permanent one and that he was crazy for having a kid in his fifties given that Tom barely had enough energy in his thirties to keep up with them," I relay. "It just kinda put into perspective that all my obsessing about Anna's youth and Dan replacing me with her and my jealousy of that isn't the healthiest to focus on. What I should be focusing on is that Dan just may have royally made a wrong turn that he will now have to deal with for the rest of his miserable life. And that while I'm sure I was definitely part of the problem with us, it wasn't all me, he doesn't exactly have the best judgement."

"Wait, Tom said that?" she asks inquisitively with a slight flinch. "About him being nuts for having a kid now at his age?"

"Yeah," I confirm. "I don't have lots of trustworthy guys in my life offering perspective on the situation, so it was good hearing it from him. But enough about Dan," I wave her off.

"Right, right," she moves her hands excitedly. "Tell me."

"So during the party Cam drives me to the train and on the platform I figure out where Brian's brother's bar is and surprise him there with no plan. I almost shit myself when I walked in and saw him talking to a woman that I thought might be a girlfriend. Turns out it was his sister-in-law. We talk, go back to his place, and turns out he is like this artisan-type wunderkind, gardener, chef, jack-of-all-trades." I pause for dramatic effect. "And one of those trades is sex. Like, he's really good at it." I burst out laughing as Debbie hangs on my every word.

"Maybe Dan was just really bad at it," Debbie jokes.

"I'll make fun of Dan all you want," I admit, "but he was actually quite good in that department. But Brian was just, I dunno, *better*. Anyway, the next morning he made me breakfast, we hung out all day, had sex yet again and then just had the sweetest day I've had in a long, long time. He actually already made a tentative plan to hang out with me again on Sunday. He's going up to northern Wisconsin with his family later this week, so he'll be out of touch for a bit."

"That's amazing Jack," Debbie gives my hand a squeeze. "I honestly can't remember when I've seen you, this, I dunno, bubbly and positive in a really long time."

"Right? I'm trying not to overthink it," I confess. "I mean, Mom's perpetual negative voice that's turned into my inner self-doubt has definitely peeked out a bit. After he left, I was like is this guy is some sort of too-good-to-be-true con artist? I mean we've all seen those news report where some unsuspecting middle-aged lady going through some shit falls for some guy who steals all her money or murders her."

"Jackie…stop," she says. "You've lived in this city long enough, if anything, I think your bullshit detector is set a little too high. You could spot someone about to scam you a mile away."

"I guess," I agree. "Though maybe the real thing I'm worried about is that he is genuinely great and will realize I'm not good enough for him."

"Oh Jack," Debbie rubs my shoulder.

"I know, I know," I sigh, "Mom really did a number on me. But this honestly…this just feels…good. Like I know it's been decades since I slept with someone new, but I remember back in my twenties the first time with a new guy was always sorta like a bad show-and-tell session. They showed off their greatest hits of moves, I showed off my greatest hits of moves, but most of the time I was so worried about what the other person was thinking or doing that I almost forgot to enjoy the act. Last night was so different. We were actually listening to each other and feeling things out in real time, like we'd known each other for years or something. And it was just so good."

"You're a helluva lot more confident and experienced than you were back then," she corrects.

"I guess," I acknowledge. "Part of it too, may be that when I was in my twenties, there was always an agenda with every guy I met. Like every first date was a vague job interview for a relationship, marriage, and all that entails. But now, I think I'm living a bit more in the present, just looking for fun and meaningful companionship and connection." I lean back smiling as Debbie stares at me.

"Did you do ayahuasca with this guy or something? You sound like some enlightened hippie. Where the fuck is my cynical sister?" she mocks looking under the couch pillow that I hit her back with.

"But I really am sorry that I made you worry and that I left the party without saying anything," I apologize.

"Seriously," she frowned, "not cool."

"I know," I agree. "But to be honest it gave me a little quality time with Cam. He's a good egg, Debs.

I don't know if I talked to him that much in years, he's always so quiet. In fact, I didn't realize he was into video game design and stuff. I feel like he definitely has more goals and plans than I do."

"He opens up to Tom much more than he does to me," she says. "I think when he sees how Maddy can be so bright, shiny, and such a big personality that he stops trying in her presence and just becomes a wall flower sometimes. He's a good kid though. He has a kind soul, which I wish more people could see. He just falls into the background if there are louder voices in the room."

"Yeah, but when he does speak, it's worth it. Like I said, don't worry about him. I think he's gonna be just fine." We sit quietly for a minute as Debbie looks around my new and improved apartment. "Soooo, million-dollar question now that we're so openly talking about our lives…have you talked to Tom yet about, you know, the whole intimacy thing?"

"You have sex once and now you're fucking Dr. Ruth?" she says defensively.

"No, no, no," I stop her. "Like I said, I chatted at the party with him and had forgotten what a good guy Tom is. Debs, he was willing to go to the Jewel for you on a Saturday morning. I love you and all, but I'm not sure I would brave a Saturday morning supermarket deli counter for you," I joke. "And he attempted to pick up our crazy-ass mother! I think he's willing to do just about anything for you. Talk to him about whatever it is you're going through or what you want."

She ignores my words and instead kisses my forehead and asks if I want to go out to grab some food because while my apartment has drastically transformed into something that looks that of an adult, my refrigerator still looks like a broke college student runs the household.

"By the way," she says as I get dressed in the bathroom, "Maddy told me to tell you that your makeover content should be going up live on Friday. I think she said it was going to be on YouTube and some Reels or stories or something. Maybe TikTok. I don't honestly know what she said. If Cam doesn't talk enough, Mads doesn't stop talking so half the time I stop listening."

"Speaking of someone who I don't listen to," I add. "Have you talked to Mom since she blew off the party?" I peek my head around the corner to see Debbie roll her eyes.

"I called her, but she sort of pretended like nothing happened. Like she didn't come because she had a headache or something. Like no mention of Tom going out there and her refusing to come with him. I don't know what's up with her," she says.

"I suspect she came to the realization that the party wasn't in her honor and she couldn't see any reason to make an effort to attend something that didn't exclusively revolve around people fawning all over her," I say sharply.

"She's getting older, Jack," Debbie starts to defend her. "I honestly think this is just who she is and no matter what we say she won't change. I think we have to love her for who she is." I raise my eyebrow disapprovingly from across the room.

"OK," I half-heartedly respond. "You first, because I'm going with the other self-help mantra of setting boundaries and protecting myself from toxic individuals."

"I should ask Maddy do a makeover on her. Mom would probably love it. She'd love to have some dude give her clip-in hair and paint on eyebrows that nearly touch her hairline." I wave the clip in hair that is sitting in my drawer in Debbie's direction.

"Ooh, you can use that for role playing with your plumber," she laughs.

Without the pressure of job hunting, man hunting, and life reorganizing, my week frees up and I feel like a lady of leisure. I take long walks along Lake Michigan, I catch up on podcasts, I go for out coffees and scroll through my phone at the corner shop, and take midday naps just because I can.

Brian texts me the night before he heads up to Wisconsin for his vacation, just to say he's thinking about me and looking forward to our meeting up on Sunday. I respond, in-kind and feel like an idiot for being smitten based on one good weekend.

Despite my best efforts to be a secure grown up, I Google him out of curiosity to see if I can discover anything else about him and his past. I find an old semi-private Facebook account, to which he hasn't posted in years. There are a few pictures of his daughters, a photo of him with his brothers where he had a goatee, and a picture of a beloved family cat that died at the ripe old age of 18 in 2011. He's tagged in several other photos that direct to the bar's Facebook page where he appears at Christmas parties and St. Patrick's Day events. Thankful that I didn't unearth an article about him being recently arrested for fraud or murder, and slightly embarrassed that I thought that was a remote possibility, I decide to put my amateur detective work to bed and be content with reality.

On Friday I go to a midday movie at the Music Box Theater, a place I haven't been to in years, to watch a double feature as part of a film noir festival. Armed with all-too-buttery popcorn and no expectations, I turn off my phone and prepare for a little black and white nostalgia. My father was a film noir enthusiast and made Debbie and I spend many a rainy Saturday afternoon when we were kids watching some of his favorites. There's something satisfying about the way the movies are shot, how you know that they will be resolved in the end, and that there's usually a clear cut good and bad guy and a lot of tough broads sprinkled in between.

Three hours, many murders, and a whole lot of plot twists later the lights come on and modern reality sets in as I notice I'm surrounded by old men and a few young hipster boys with twirly mustaches. I also realize that my shirt is covered in popcorn remnants and butter grease that will likely require special washing interventions. I step outside blinded by the afternoon sun and slightly confused that the world is no longer in black and white.

Walking to the bus I turn my phone on to check the schedule and am met with hundreds of Instagram notifications. I haven't posted anything in months so my first thought is that my account has been hacked. I click on the app and encounter nasty comments, DMs, and reactions from strangers and accounts I don't follow. Confused I scroll and realize that I've been tagged in a reel by MadLove. I'd forgotten that Debbie said today would be the release day for my makeover content. I also notice I have a text from Debbie.

> Sister Debbie: Jackie, I'm so sorry. I'm trying to get ahold of Maddy, but can't

reach her. I didn't know she was going to do that.

Sister Debbie: Where are you? Are you OK?

Me: Was in a movie? What's going on? Do what?

Within seconds Debbie calls me.

"Have you not seen the YouTube video?" she asks frantically. "It was posted a couple of hours ago."

"No," I reply. "I was at the Music Box in a movie. I came out and have all these Instagram things going on that I haven't even looked at. What's going on Deb? You're scaring me."

"Oh God, Jack," she sounds worried. "I'm so sorry."

"Sorry about what!" I ask emphatically. "Debbie, what's going on?"

"So, I guess when you and Maddy went back to your apartment after the whole big makeover reveal thing she or her team or someone left a camera rolling in your apartment. Do they even call it rolling if it's a phone? I dunno..." she is distracted.

"Debbie?!!"

"She recorded a video of you making fun of Brian the plumber and saying some not great things about Reed Publishing and posted it on YouTube as part of the makeover content."

"What?" I whisper in disbelief.

"It looks kinda like you and Maddy were just having a conversation that she sorta caught on tape," Deb explains. "But she included some of it at the end of the video. Maddy used it as part of this sorta commercial sponsor thing that says something like the MadLove team made magic happen on the outside but sometimes it takes a lot more work to fix someone's insides. That's why I turn to RemoteTherapy and then she does a whole therapy plug."

"But Debbie," I try to rack my brain. "I don't remember saying anything bad about Brian! Like I may have said I wasn't sure if he liked me or something like that, but I don't know what else I said? And I for sure don't remember saying anything about the company…Fuck…what did she do?"

"I dunno, Jack, but I'm not gonna sugar coat it, it's not good. Sit down when you watch it," she says. "I'm not sure where she is at the moment, but if I get in touch with her, I'll see if I can make her take it down. The Instagram reel doesn't have that bit in it as far as I can tell."

"Lemme go and check this out," I say. "Call me back if you talk to Maddy."

"It's gonna be OK, Jackie," she says unconvincingly before I hang up on her.

I sit on a bench near the park, put in my

ear buds and navigate to the MadLove channel. The cover image of her latest video is a picture of Maddy's perfectly made-up face next to mine where I look half asleep and disheveled at the start of the makeover, the video title is "Can MadLove Makeover a Middle-aged Mess?"

I press play and look around to make sure no one is watching me watch myself, in a self-conscious way that only Gen X seems to care about. The first 10 minutes of the 13-minute video proceeds as one would expect. There are some quick cuts of me spinning around before and then after my hair salon visit with the frightening long hair. Maddy interviews Darwin and he plugs the sale of his hair extensions. Then the makeup bit follows suit, with a before, after, and an interview and mini commercial for the line of cosmetics they used on me. The clothing segment features a shot of the package of clothing I was given with Maddy describing the process of setting up a profile and style guide online. Then there's a quick cut of me coming out wearing the outfit where they seem to have chopped my head out of the frame so you can't see me laughing or making fun of the clothes. Maddy then provides guidance on finding your style in a voiceover and there is a video of her playing around with the web site.

While not exactly the most flattering portrayal of myself, it is what it is and I'm not seeing anything remotely troubling. After the YouTube commercial, the video proceeds from Maddy's point of view as she is the one filming. We enter my apartment revealing the flooding, the panicking team, and Brian wearing his work shirt with the company's logo. The audio for this section of the video is muted and you just hear Maddy providing narration for what has happened. She explains the flood, but glosses over it and instead pans into all the details of the apartment that her team has improved upon. It is so smoothly done that unless you were actually in the apartment at that point you wouldn't have known that Arlo and Riff were melting down and my building management company was off to the side demanding insurance information.

When she's done giving a curated tour of the apartment, Maddy focuses the camera's gaze on Brian and the back of my head. He's seen smiling and talking to me with his body ever so slightly leaning into mine. He sees the camera and waves in an overexaggerated manor at Maddy in the way that people in home videos always did in the 1980s. You don't hear our conversation, but instead hear Maddy providing voiceover that was added after the fact.

"Brian, the plumber, is clearly flirting with Jackie. Now that Jackie is single and looking for love, I'm never one to miss making a MadLove connection," she says. The screen turns black with words on it, *"When asked if she'd consider dating Brian…"*

The next clip of video is from another angle, presumably from a camera hidden somewhere on my windowsill without my knowledge. It shows me, in my ridiculous makeover attire.

"Brian? He is just a dude," I appear to say. I then walk around in a circle like an ape making mocking gestures with my hands and body. "One of those big, lumbering, loud Chicago guys who, you know, probably spends the weekends watching sports, mowing his lawn, and grilling meat. You know, like a dude, just like plodding through life sorta content to just be, I dunno, ordinary. Like the equivalent of my job at Reed Publishing, just sorta uninventive and 'basic' something you have to do, but don't want to do. Like a dude's fine to chat with on the bus or at the neighborhood block party, but one day you'll just be sitting on the couch and think, is this what I've chosen for my life?"

The video then cuts to Maddy sitting on the couch in her loft apartment. "Do you ever feel like Jackie? Stuck in your ways, unable to see opportunity right in front of you? Do you find yourself judging others harshly because that's how you judge yourself? Are you stuck in a job or a company that you hate? Do you need to get out of your own head? By using the code MadLove10, you can get ten percent off your first conversation with a RemoteTherapy therapist. I love RemoteTherapy, because you get matched with a licensed therapist who you can text, call, or interact with the way you love best. I MadLove you all and it's time for you to MadLove yourselves. And if we can get Jackie to find some MadLove in the future I'll be sure to share an update. Now don't forget to like this video and subscribe to my channel, and I'm wishing you all MadLove in your life." The video ends.

I want to throw up. My hands start shaking and I really do wonder if all the popcorn I shoved down in the movie theater may return to see the light of day. Maddy secretly recorded our private conversation and edited random bits of it together so it seems like I'm giving a cruel and convincing-sounding monologue about how I find Brian repulsive. I remember saying the words used in the video, but I said them with much more context as I explained being embarrassed that that had been my first assumption of him, how wrong I realized I was, and how I definitely did feel something between us but didn't act on it because my self-esteem was in the toilet. She'd deliberately cut out those parts of the conversation. On top of that, she included a snippet of video where I'm making disparaging remarks about the company that actually agreed to take me back and pay me. The craziest part is that she apparently did all of this in an effort to generate money from a sponsor whose sole mission is to support *mental health*.

The editing looks completely smooth, so smooth in fact that had I not been in the room, I myself wouldn't question if the video was real and shot in one continuous moment. What the hell was she thinking and what the hell am I gonna do?

The comments on the video are numerous ranging from people randomly professing their love of Maddy to those harshly criticizing my looks, personality, age, weight, generation, and everything in between. Someone named UBetZa wrote "Good of you to try MadLove, but there is no helping Boomers." Another person named KarmaMama wrote "I can't believe THAT woman criticized THAT guy, did you see her? She shouldn't judge anyone." Further down someone called RunningRay said "That guy dodged a bullet with having to deal with a hot mess Karen. She deserves to be ugly and have no job." On and on the comments pour in and my feelings of nausea grow as I read each one.

As I scroll, Instagram notifications continue to chime and buzz. Scrolling through, the hashtag "TeamBrian" appears to be attributed to posts as is "GenXJackAss." The content with Brian didn't even appear in the Instagram reel, but Maddy's loyal followers feel the need to comment on it in all platforms. My heart is pounding in my ears and I start to sweat profusely.

My phone rings from an unknown number and my first thought is that Brian somehow saw the video at his cabin and is calling from a Wisconsin landline.

"I'm so sorry," I say straight away.

"Is this Jacqueline Novak?" A woman's voice asks.

"Yes, this is Jackie," I say skeptically.

"Jackie, this is Rhonda Burns from Steinhoff, Bergen, and Johnson," she pauses. "The law firm handling your employment case."

"Right, right," I reply. "I'm so sorry, I have a bunch of things going on at the moment. Of course, I remember you."

"Well, those things are probably why I am calling," she says matter-of-factly. "We got a call a few moments ago from your employer, Reed Publishing, about the contract position that they had agreed to extend to you. It has been brought to their attention that you were featured in a popular influencer's YouTube video slandering the company's name. Do you know what I'm referring to? The influencer was…"

"MadLove," I respond. I look up to my right to see a couple of teenagers laughing at some video on their phone and I immediately assume they are laughing at me. I tilt my head down like a celebrity hiding in plain sight as I continue my conversation.

"Yes," she agrees. "Then you know what I am talking about."

"It's my niece," I clarify. "She asked me to take part in some makeover content creation for her and then unbeknownst to me filmed private conversations and edited them together without context in an unflattering way. I'll admit it wasn't my finest moment, but I'm not sure I would call it slanderous." I think having a job at a textbook publisher is the definition of basic and not-cutting edge. Did I really tell the world something that they didn't already know?

"Well unfortunately," she adds, "sometimes slander can be in the eyes of the beholder. In this instance, Reed Publishing would like to rescind the contract employment offer and cut ties with you."

"Right," I say knowingly defeated.

"I would advise you to let it go given the circumstances," she says. "Of course, the decision is up to you, and if you'd like us to counter or pursue other action we can discuss it further."

"No, Rhonda," I shake my head. "This is a done deal. I get where they're coming from."

"I'm sorry this didn't work out better," she says. "I wish you the best of luck in whatever comes next for you and please always keep us in mind if you have any legal employment questions in the future."

I hang up, stunned, and steaming. My feelings of nausea transform into feelings of rage. I call Debbie back, and tears that I can't control stream down my face.

"What has she done, Deb?" I squeak when I hear her pick up. "Reed Publishing saw the video and I just lost my job. I lost my fucking JOB. AGAIN! And Brian is up in a cabin without Internet, but I'm bound to lose any chance with him once he sees it. Does Maddy hate me or something? Or is she just that dumb?"

"Jackie, oh Jesus Christ, I'm so sorry, hon," Debbie is beside herself. "I think she, and the people she works with, are just so used to doing these types of things for these sponsors or whatever they probably all weren't thinking."

"I get that," I say, "but the consequences of her actions just destroyed my fucking life. Not to mention there are hundreds of her followers sending me horrible messages saying horrible things. Who sends people death threats over a 5-minute video that was supposed to be about hair and makeup?"

"Honey, I'm so sorry," she replies.

"What do I do, Deb?" I ask. "Where's Maddy, can I get her to take this thing down before it does even more damage?"

"I was able to get in touch with Janelle," she says. "Maddy was in a meeting. It sounds like they are about to leave to do some sort of live event thing at Navy Pier later this afternoon."

"OK thanks," I hang up.

Debbie immediately calls back, but I don't pick up. I go to Instagram and delete my account as if wiping the app off my phone will stop the hatred coming my way. I get up, dab my face with my sleeve, put on my sunglasses and proceed to walk to the downtown Red Line station at Addison.

At the station there are swarms of baseball fans wearing CUBS jerseys, many already quite intoxicated despite it being only late afternoon. I watch as one man props up another who has clearly spent the better part of the last hour vomiting based on the state of his face and his terribly stained shirt. This is what people who view Maddy's video will believe I think of Brian. That he's some sort of sloppy, drunken, Neanderthal, who you have to avoid on the train. Tears start to stream down my face, which one drunken CUBS fan mistakes as being related to sports.

"It's OK, we'll get 'em next time," he yells.

I wave, overcome with emotion and get on the train that pulls in. Since I deleted the only social media app I had, I have no idea where exactly Maddy might be. I also have no idea what exactly I might say if I find her. I just need to be able to confront her face-to-face to see why she thought what she did was remotely a good idea and try to get the video taken down before it does any more damage.

Swirling within my own head, I lose track of time and am downtown in the Loop before I know it. I get off the train and start the march eastward toward Navy Pier, getting angrier and angrier with every step and as each group of clueless tourists nearly knock into me with scooters, bikes, and souvenir paraphernalia. When I finally arrive at Navy Pier, I roam the periphery looking for Maddy's entourage like a frantic mother looking for a lost child. Within moments I realize that this is the equivalent of looking for a needle in a haystack, as there are multiple versions of Maddy-types filming themselves from various angles. I decide to stop moving and instead grab a seat and drink at a windowed bar to calm my nerves as I watch swarms of people walking by hoping to see her.

Debbie keeps calling and texting and I do my best to ignore it.

> Sister Debbie: Jackie, please pick up. It's going to be alright. We'll figure this out. Please call me back, you shouldn't be alone right now.

> Sister Debbie: Call me!

> Sister Debbie: I'm begging you Jack, just let me know you are OK. I texted Maddy, she said she'll get back to me after her event at the Navy Pier Rooftop Terrace.

Like a movie assassin who gets activated, I finish my drink and proceed to the Rooftop Terrace. Looking around I see lots of young people milling about wearing lanyards and badges. They all have entourages similar to Maddy's with cameras, multiple cell phones, and stern looks on their faces as if they're ushering around foreign dignitaries at the United Nations instead of YouTube sensations at a Chicago tourist site. There is security leading into the main event room where a person in an official looking outfit is scanning badges as groups of people go in.

I'm hopeful Maddy is fashionably late as always so that I haven't missed her before she's made her entrance. I stand behind a roped off area surrounded by YouTube fans less than half my age hoping to get a glimpse of their favorite stars who I never heard of. All the young women going into the event are covered in thick makeup with slightly inflated lips, eyebrows that appear to be drawn on by a cartoonist, and long hair that almost certainly is not their own. Their young male counterparts look like they are all sponsored exclusively by track suit and sneaker manufacturers. While I know my generation was often depicted and perceived as a bunch of despondent mopes in the 1990s, to me, this cross section of young twenty-somethings looks like a bunch of vapid dolls-come-to-life created by merchandisers.

After nearly a half an hour I assume my mission to be fruitless or perhaps Debbie, knowing me so well, decided to throw me off the trail by giving me the wrong location. Then I hear it.

"We MadLove you Maddy!!!" yells someone to my right. I look over and see a group of young girls turning around to get selfies with Maddy. She is dressed in a neon pink jumpsuit and Janelle and Xyla are behind her filming and looking like they may act as her security if anyone gets too close. Maddy slowly makes her way down the line, smiling, flashing peace signs, and dutifully taking photos with her fans. When she approaches my area, I push in front of the people standing in front of me and belly up to the velvet rope.

"Why did you do it Madeline? Why did you use your powerful platform where you pretend to be spreading love, a concept that you've never experienced or even understand, to destroy my life and my chance at happiness in 30 seconds? I know you've said this is all fake and you are just doing it for the money, but to sell out your own aunt, someone who has unconditionally loved you since the day you were born is beyond anything I can fathom."

"Aunt Jackie," she whispers truly taken aback. Steam coming out of my ears, I notice everyone in the crowd now has their cell phones pointing in my direction.

"You secretly recorded our private conversation, which I don't even think is legal, and then edited random bits together to create a whole new narrative without any context to serve the needs of a sponsor who is promoting MENTAL HEALTH? Your narcissistic selfish act has cost me my job. And no doubt it will cost me the chance at any kind of relationship with the first guy in years who has made me laugh, smile, and fucking orgasm like I've never orgasmed before!!!" I spit. Maddy stares at me white as a ghost, likely still processing that I was even standing in front of her.

"The thing is, Maddy," I continue with abandon, "My generation -- and that's Gen X not Boomer for all of you young people who seem so freakin' hurt when people use imprecise language for you but can't take two seconds to educate yourself on the generations you're insulting -- we're used to people ignoring us, forgetting us, and treating us like crap. We were raised to realize we weren't special and to behave like insults just bounce off of us, even though they chip away at our insides. But we also have empathy for others, can admit when we're wrong, and have the ability to change our minds because we know down to our souls that everything in the world isn't binary and black and white. Not everyone has your privilege to make a living doing what they want to do, and not everyone immediately knows that the person who could be the next great love of their life is standing right in front of them. Some of us take a minute to figure that out and your stupid and cruel fake art project of a channel that feeds into cancel culture just cancelled my livelihood, likely any chance at a relationship with Brian, and basically me, one of the people who loves you most in this world."

"Jackie," Janelle whispers, "we're live." She points to the camera and I'm not sure if she's suggesting that I turn to face it more head on or turn away and pretend nothing happened. Either way I continue undeterred.

"I don't care, Janelle," I respond. "I live in the real world where everything is always live. Maddy needs to start living in that world too where she isn't a puppet for corporate sponsors and people who don't care about her. Do you realize she's said she's never actually even been in love? And she's trying to sell that to everyone who follows her?" Maddy flashes me a look as if I just told the world she has a third nipple.

"Take the video down, Maddy," I implore. "This isn't you. I know you are an amazing person on the inside, and I think your fans would actually love you more if you were the real you."

Maddy either doesn't know what to do or say, or plans to face the camera and double down on me being crazy and in need of psychological help the moment. Since she doesn't appear to want to address me directly, I walk away. I walk away as nearly a hundred cell phone cameras turn to watch me go. I know that my outburst will likely just be dismissed as the act of a Karen gone wild on some beloved YouTuber's channel, but I have nothing left to lose. The video is out there and I'm sure after these clips end up wherever all these people put them, it will garner even more traction. Honestly, I'm just hoping to have gotten through to Maddy.

I turn off my phone, board the L back home, and for the 20-minute ride home, I am completely numb.

When I walk in my door the gravity of what has happened fully hits me and I start uncontrollably sobbing. I release buckets of tears representing the possibility of a new and improved life and in the process also release the feeling of trust and safety I had for Maddy. After a good old-fashioned cry, I sit quietly for a few moments staring at my phone as if it is a red-hot coal that I am afraid to touch because whenever I do, I get burned. However, I do turn it back on as I know there is one phone call I have to make to try to stem the consequences of what has happened.

Notifications abound when the screen comes alive, all are from Debbie except one.

> Brian: Hey there sexy – in town picking up firewood and was able to score a bar of

> cell service. Just wanted to say hi! Have a good weekend and looking forward to seeing you Sunday!

I start crying again knowing that up at his cabin Brian is still blissfully unaware of the shitstorm that awaits when he's made aware of that video. Right now he doesn't hate me and is still basking in the glow of our weekend, and I am about to break his heart several times over.

> Sister Debbie: Jackie I'm watching this live, what the hell are you doing?!!!

> Sister Debbie: You're gonna get Maddy CANCELLED!!! You told the world her whole channel is fake!

> Sister Debbie: I know you are hurt but she's just a kid – What have you done?! You are the grown up!!

My grief is fully in the anger stage and I can't even begin to process Debbie's messages and consider anyone's feelings other than my own.

> Me: She's 23 and will likely get a sponsorship deal out of all this, I AM THE ONE WHO IS CANCELLED and will forever be known as #GenXJackAss So fuck you for defending her! I guess she learned how to live a fake life from

YOU who can't even talk to your own HUSBAND!

After hitting send, I rummage through the kitchen cabinet to find the bottle with the type of weed gummy that I'd bought during the time I was in peak divorce meltdown. The pot barista, salesperson, or better yet, stoner behind the counter convinced me that it supposedly helps calm anxiety. I pop one of those in my mouth, sit on the couch and try to figure out how I'm going to make this call. After reciting words that sound like I'm practicing lines as an actor about to take part in a tragic stage production, I dial Brian's number.

"Hi this is Brian, you know what to do, I'll call you back," the sound of his voice on his voicemail message makes my practiced monologue escape my brain.

"Hey Brian, it's Jackie. Ummm…yeah. I know you probably won't get this message until you're heading home on Sunday. But honestly that's probably a good thing, because I don't want to interrupt your vacation. And I hope you're having an amazing time. But I need to give you a heads up about something that will probably land on your radar as soon as you hit civilization." I pause and wonder if the voicemail is picking up the sound of my loudly beating heart. "So Maddy posted a video on her channel with my makeover thing, but at the end of it included a video she created from random bits of a private conversation she secretly taped with me. It looks like she did this so that she could get the video sponsored by an online therapy site. The content is," my voice starts to shake, "about you."

Tears start streaming down my face and my rambling doesn't remotely resemble what I thought I would say in this message. "The way it's edited together, it looks and sounds like I am making fun of you and is just otherwise cruel and repulsive. I know you have no reason to trust me after just one weekend, but I beg you to believe that I never said all those things collectively in a sentence. It'll be hard to believe when you see it, the editing is impeccable. I mean, even I can't tell that she edited clips together and I was actually in the room, but please know that that was not me. I mean it's me, but, well…you know. I've confronted Maddy to get her to take it down, and am probably even more cancelled than when I started since everyone with a cell phone was watching. In fact, I lost my job, again. But I think my biggest worry is that I've lost my chance with you. Though if that's the case, I completely understand because I don't know that I would take a chance on me after seeing that either. All of this rambling is to say, geez…fuck… is that I'm sorry. I'm so, so sorry. I know it is just early days for us, but I hope this isn't the end of those days…Fuck…OK…yeah." I hang up.

I have no idea what I just said, but am pretty

sure that if the video didn't make me sound like a lunatic, that voicemail most certainly did. I start crying again knowing that any chance with Brian is likely over and I'm pretty much back to square one. No job, no man, no support from my sister and best friend, and there is a very good chance that prospects for all of those categories are forever ruined as my name, face, and antics live on in Google-able Internetville forever. After a significant period of crying, I feel the gummy taking effect. I take a long hot shower and just crawl into bed hoping that today's nightmare will magically turnaround tomorrow.

With social media apps deleted I adhere to strict self-preservation directive to not Google myself. As such, my phone sits silently untouched on the table for nearly two days as if it is social and mental kryptonite. During this time, I don't receive any text messages from Debbie, or Maddy, nor anyone else. At first, I wonder if they just got the hint and are plotting a grand apology. However, then I begin to worry that things somehow started to blow up even further and I am just ignorantly and blissfully unaware. By Sunday afternoon, any false sense of calm that I had tricked myself into conjuring starts to rotate in the air like a summer tornado threatening to uproot my life.

My initial "has he heard my voicemail and seen the video" panic begins to swirl around lunchtime. I assume Brian's phone would likely pick up service soon after they left their cabin's dead zone. As the minutes then hours tick by without any word from him, I don't know what to think. Had my voicemail message even fully recorded? It was so long, perhaps it got cut off or didn't save? Do I send a follow up text?

Even my own brain can detect the optimistic lies that I am trying to tell myself. The realistic me then steps in. Did he see the video and block my number? Should I call him back and try to talk to him directly? Do I show up at his house with a Boombox over my head like Lloyd Dobler? I feel like a 15-year-old girl instead of a 52-year-old woman. Without Debbie as my sounding board and voice of reason, I feel like I'm flying emotionally solo without a safety net. I settle on doing nothing, assuming that if he hadn't received the message or the video he'll reach out as planned and I can have a second try to right my wrongs. On the flip side, if he indeed had received everything, maintaining my distance at least wouldn't add to the impression that I'm lunatic stalker. Either way, the only thing I can really do is sit, do nothing, and wait.

By ten at night, tears are once again streaming down my face as a Mazzy Star album plays in the background serving to rub auditory salt into my heartbreaking wounds. A half an hour later my phone buzzes with a text and I bolt upright with fear.

> Brian: I don't even know where to start. I need time and space. Please respect that.

I pour over the words in his brief text as if I am trying to decode a message that impacts national security. Does that mean he's not throwing away all future possibility? If he was, he would just tell me to go to hell, or ghost me, right? Or maybe this *is* his polite way of telling me he's throwing away all future possibility? How do I respond? Do I respond? I need to acknowledge that I've seen the message, but if I write anything back, would he consider this as not respecting his need for space? Do I just give it a thumbs up emoji? Or is that passive aggressive? Fuck.

I have the wherewithal to refrain from typing anything in the actual message as I play my internal game of what do I do ping pong, so as not make those little dots appear and disappear on his end. Instead, like any sane person, I go to Reddit and try to find a similar topic. I type in "How do I respond to a text where someone says they need space?" The answers are endless and vary to align with every thought that just ran through in my head. I settle on a short message back.

> Me: I understand and will honor your

wishes. I'm so very sorry.

I re-read it six times before sending it off and immediately regret my phrasing the moment I hit send. "Honor your wishes?" That sounds like something someone says when referring to someone's funeral or will. Ugh. I stare at my phone and the text chain for a full 15 minutes hoping to see little dots appear as if my words were profound enough to inspire a reply. Of course, nothing else pops up and I am left feeling empty and even more alone than when I started.

TEN

I plod through the week continuing to ensure that I don't Google myself while I apply to every job imaginable. Barista in training, entry level editor, executive level editor, restaurant hostess, building management receptionist, retail space manager, traditional and digital publishing jobs, jobs that offer a full suite of benefits, and then jobs that offer no benefits. Remote jobs, onsite jobs, and hybrid locations, I tailor, revise, and fire off resumes, re-input my resume into portals, and click apply on LinkedIn as needed. I am the job equivalent of a creepy guy on a dating app casting a wide swiping net in hopes of getting some unsuspecting suitor to respond.

I also reach out to Liz, who obviously had heard what happened, as the news of my Internet performance spread like office folklore. She offers the perfunctory "I'll let you know if I hear anything" reply, but I know that she can't recommend me for anything even if something appropriate does come up as vouching for me could negatively impact her reputation. I don't blame her.

By Thursday afternoon, after hearing nothing on the job front, nothing from Brian, nothing from Debbie and nothing from Maddy and her team, any optimism lurking deep below the surface melts away and I start to panic. It's then that I break my self-imposed personal quarantine and Google myself to find a shitstorm of content. The original makeover video has been taken down, as far as I can tell, however there is no new video or response from Maddy. When I look up my name there are nearly fifty versions of my yelling at her video from various angles. Having been in a bit of a fugue state of rage when I encountered her, I'm shocked by seeing it again with more clarity. Various Maddy look-alikes offer context around the video ranging from, as expected, me being a bully Karen, to Maddy being the inappropriate bully, to others begging for everyone to just tone down the social media rhetoric, as if Maddy and I are national leaders, while they simultaneously implore viewers to like and subscribe to their channels.

As I start to become engrossed in reading the comments, I feel my blood start to boil. Rather than engage with the trolls as every fiber of my being would love to do, I decide to self soothe in a way I haven't in years.

♦ ♦ ♦

An hour later I walk into the Art Institute of Chicago. It's surprisingly busy for a weekday afternoon and I am happy to see that in an online world full of so much vitriol, there are still so many people seeking out beautiful and interesting things in real life. Looking around the lobby, I realize I haven't been in the building in years. Like many city dwellers who have the best of everything at their doorstep, in recent years I barely venture beyond the ten-block radius of my apartment unless I have a specific need to.

I purchase a ticket and start to leaf through the exhibit brochure.

"Jackie Novak?" I hear in the distance. I look up and see a tall and striking Black woman walking toward me. She has short impeccably styled hair, oversized bright red round glasses, and is wearing a suit and bright red stilettos. My mind races and I scan her face trying to place how I may know her. When she gets closer, I can see her name badge, but still can't figure it out.

"Oh my God, Jackie!" she exclaims. I worry that perhaps this woman saw my altercation with Maddy online and is about to call me out on it in public. My uncertainty must be plastered on my face as she stops short of making physical contact with me. "It's me, Darlene. I'm Darlene

Washington now, but it used to be Darlene James. Rogers Park? Class of…"

"Holy crap, DARLENE!" The lightbulb of recognition finally ignites and I move forward and hug her. Darlene and I bonded when we were in the ninth grade - we were two of the tallest girls in our class who had absolutely no interest in sports but were hounded relentlessly about why we weren't on the basketball or volleyball teams. "It's been…"

"Girl, don't even," she laughs. "Thirty-five years or thereabouts?"

"You look fantastic," I say sincerely. "Do you work here?"

"On the administration side," she explains. "I'm not usually even in this part of the museum, but we have some donors and delegates coming in today, so I came down to greet them and take them up. Put on the dog and pony show. I've been here for nearly 20 years now."

"That's amazing," I reply.

"And you?" she asks. "Weren't you going to go into something art related? I always remember you drawing and hanging out in the art room back in school."

"Good memory," I acknowledge. "I did get an art history degree after high school, but went off and became an editor for a number of years. Unfortunately, I'm in between things at the moment – I got laid off recently, so," I pause and laugh somewhat uncomfortably, "if you guys need anyone around here, let me know. I'll dust the art, point people toward the bathroom, edit art descriptions. At this point I'm not picky."

"Seriously?" she asks. "Here, take my card and send me a resume. The job market is so tough right now, I feel like it's impossible to get a leg up anywhere. We're always looking for good people. My office is across the hall from the Director of HR, I'll happily pass it along."

"That would be incredible, Darlene," I smile profusely. "Thank you so much."

"Of course," she clasps my hand. "We tall gals of Rogers Park gotta stick together. Is your family still in town?"

"My mom is still in the same house I grew up in," I admit. "My dad passed away about 10 years ago, and my sister Debbie, not sure if you remember her, she's up in Evanston. I'm over in Wicker Park. So we're still all in Chicagoland in some capacity. How about you?"

"I have two sons, both went to college in Atlanta, and then they stayed down there after they graduated," she beams. "They're smarter than me and bailed on the Chicago winters. My parents retired down to Florida and have been down there for a while now. And my brother Kenny, do you remember him?" I nod my head, mentally running through the pages of my high school yearbook. "He's still in town. He's down in Hyde Park working for U of Chicago."

"That's amazing, Darlene," I smile. She looks past me toward the front door and her face changes to a broad smile as she waves at someone in the distance.

"I gotta go, girl," she says. "Duty calls. It was so good seeing you after all this time. And I mean what I said, send that resume and we'll find something that's a good fit."

"You're the best, Darlene," I say. "Thanks so much and say hi to your parents and brother for me." She leans in for a hug and pats my arm as she walks toward the entrance to greet a group of suited individuals. She swipes her badge at the front area and lets out an easy laugh engaging with this small and seemingly powerfully moneyed crowd.

I instinctively pull my phone out of my bag to text Debbie and tell her who I ran into, but as soon as I do reality sets back in and I remember we're not speaking. Feeling forlorn, I show my entrance ticket and finally enter the museum. I wander around viewing new exhibits that showcase artists I've never heard of as well as those I've admired for years. I allow myself a momentary fantasy of thinking about what it might be like to actually work in a place like this, a place I could actually be proud and excited to work at. The idea feels like a dream, one that I don't want to get too excited about because as of late my dreams tend to turn into nightmares quite quickly.

The museum is massive and beyond the inspirational art on the walls, the building allows for breathtaking and contemplative glimpses of downtown Chicago from picture windows lurking around every corner. Stuck in my own little world and my own swirling head as of late, I forget how magical this area can be to walk around. For a brief moment, I forget about all the drama that has been surrounding me and just stand there admiring what my little world is and what could be.

I ultimately make my way downstairs in the museum to the Thorne Miniature rooms, a collection of dioramas crossed with doll-less dollhouses that showcase interior design throughout history. Debbie and I were always fascinated by the rooms, making our father take us to this section of the museum first and foremost every time we visited as kids. As I walk around today, the rooms seem even smaller than they did back then, but are no less magical than when I first saw them. I see a pair of young sisters standing on the brass rail in front of one of the rooms peering in and commenting on all the details inside, much like we used to do. Their father tends to their younger brother melting down in spectacular fashion on the floor behind them. In watching this scene unfold, part of me wants to melt down like that little kid as I think back about how much has changed for good and bad since I was in pigtails innocently staring into the glass-cased miniature worlds.

When I get home later that evening, I pull out Darlene's card and draft a kind and professional e-mail to accompany my resume. Fearing that I sound desperate having acknowledged when I saw her that I'd be willing to dust the art or point people in the direction of the bathroom, I attempt to reign in my level of desperation by citing that I'd be happy to discuss a broad range of opportunities in which my varied skillset may align. I laugh a bit thinking about how Darlene knew me back when my skillset was carving my name into the school library table and showing boys how I could snort lines of Pixy Stix powder up my nose as if it were cocaine. While she has clearly amassed many marketable skills since then, I stop and wonder if the same can be said of me.

I send off the e-mail and then turn back toward my phone. In hopes that my chance encounter with Darlene signifies that tides are finally turning in my favor, I open my messaging app and once again stare at the last text I got from Brian in futile hope that the infamous typing dots appear. They don't.

The weekend passes by brutally slowly. The

longest I'd previously stopped talking to Debbie for was probably about eight hours and that is only because she was sleeping. It's like we're having a modern version of a staring contest, where any type of phone contact will be counted as a blink. I know I'll have to crack and apologize at some point, but I feel too hurt and broken for that point to be in the next few days.

To get out of my own head and literally get out of my small apartment, I pass the time by taking long walks to random destinations in the city. If all this drama has been good for anything, it can be said that it's helping to improve my waistline. Being too depressed and broke to overeat and filling long stretches of time with walks, I feel the pounds slipping away with minimal effort. As I walk, if I make eye contact with anyone under the age of 30, I panic that they might recognize me from the MadLove YouTube debacle. Of course, these feelings are unfounded as I soon realize that I'm invisible to anyone under the age of the 30 - simply another middle-aged woman with nothing to say or akin to their mom as they glorify the 1990s fashions that I wore the first time around.

On Sunday, on my way home from a four-hour afternoon walk, I break my recent self-imposed rule forbidding the purchase of expensive artisan coffee. I stop into my regular coffee shop to make small talk with the barista, realizing that I haven't actually used my voice to talk to another human being in the past 48 hours.

"Hey Miles," I say. "I didn't realize you did weekend afternoons? I thought you were only weekdays. I haven't been in like a whole week and the whole world and schedule has gone topsy turvy." I laugh at my own dad joke as I realize I am speed talking like someone who has already had too many coffees in the day or someone who has not had a conversation with another human being in far too long.

"Hey Jackie," he says quietly. His eyes dart to the right and he's subtly pushing his chin in the same direction. I hold eye contact with him like a dog trying to read a person's thoughts.

"Everything OK, Miles?" I ask. Is he having a seizure? Has he taken drugs?

"Yeah, yeah," he continues and then makes the same move with his eyes and chin again.

"Oh my god, is this place being held up? Blink a few times if you need me to run outside and call 911," I whisper, genuinely concerned, without moving my mouth.

"I think he's trying to tell you that I'm sitting here," a booming voice says from a table against the wall. I look up at Miles and he blinks slowly before shrugging and going off to make my coffee. I turn around and see Brian sitting at the table with a drink. He's wearing jeans and a black t-shirt and I'm struck by how attracted I am to him when I look in his direction.

My heart immediately sinks and I don't know if I should go over and sit with him or run out the door. While the majority of people sitting in the small shop are wearing headphones and typing on laptops or tablets, Brian's silence-piercing voice and my reaction akin to a cat being caught eating a houseplant has made their eyes dart towards us as their heads turn in curiosity. I approach his table completely unsure of what may ensue.

"Hey," I say sheepishly. I walk across the coffee shop to where he's sitting and I can hear my heart pounding in my ears similarly to how it sounded when I left that tragic rambling voicemail message while he was away.

"Hey," he replies, making only mild eye contact and staring into his coffee.

"I can go," I offer. "I fully understand if you need space. I honestly didn't realize you would be here," I pause. "I mean, actually, why are you here?" He gestures for me to sit down and I do, slowly as if any sudden moves could inspire him to change his mind.

Miles walks over to the table and hands me the coffee that I can't remember if I even paid for. In all the time that I have been coming to this shop, I don't think he has ever brought anyone a drink to their table. Either we look like we're in a sad state, or he saw the MadLove video and is eagerly awaiting a front row seat to the soap opera that he assumes will unfold.

"I'm here," Brian says slowly, "to sort out what's next and if I really want to talk to you. I mean, I think I want to talk to you, but I'm not sure. I went over to your building, with the intent of talking to you. But when I got there, I stood in front of the front door for a minute before chickening out. I came in here instead and had two coffees while I try to decide what to do. And let me tell you these high-octane coffees give you a false sense of clarity on many things." By the tone of his voice, I couldn't tell what that clarity might be.

"I know my words probably mean shit right now, but if they do mean anything, I would love it if you talked to me," I confess. My voice is shaky like when I was a kid and had to tell my parents I got a bad grade on a test. He takes a long sip from his drink. I can't even bear to bring my drink to my lips as I'm afraid if I ingest anything at the moment I'll throw up.

"I got your message when I was driving home from the cabin," he explains, now looking directly in my eyes. "My daughters were in the car with me. All weekend, without even meaning to, I'd been talking about you and hyping you up. I was saying things like I'd met this woman who is kinda quirky, funny, and cute. I explained how you came to the bar and sought me out. My eldest daughter, Kendra, said I actually seemed kinda, you know giddy." He takes a sip of his coffee as I can see him reliving the moment in real time. "Then I get your message, which plays over speakerphone in the car. A car with both my daughters in it." I put my hand over my mouth, and Brian shakes his head acknowledging that my perception of the horror of that scenario is correct. "So while your message is finishing, Melissa, my younger daughter is in the back seat and pulls up the video on Maddy's page. The two girls are watching it at full volume while I'm trying not to drive us straight into a ditch."

"Oh my God, Brian. I'm so sorry," I touch his hand and am pleasantly surprised that he doesn't immediately pull it away.

"After watching it, both girls start Googling, while badmouthing you and telling me to cut ties with you. They think that you just spent the weekend with me as a publicity stunt, like a dare so that Maddy's YouTube channel could get more views. Meanwhile your words just keep echoing in my head." I start to open my mouth, but stay silent owing him the courtesy and space to say whatever he came here to say. "Kendra then finds the video of you losing your shit at Maddy. At that point I'd pulled over at a rest stop to figure out what the hell was going on. I will say, hearing you tell the world how I make you orgasm was quite... interesting," he smirks. "Though watching it with my daughters was awkward as hell."

"Fuck," I sigh mortifyingly.

"Yeah," he agrees.

"Fuck," I gasp again, nearly speechless. "You do know though that it was all a meticulous editing job on the part of Maddy and her team, right? I didn't actually say those things about you. I'll be honest, and say that maybe the very first time I saw you I might have wondered or assumed you were just some sort of stereotypical dumb jock type, but that thought was so fleeting and disproven the moment we started talking." He puts his hand up and shakes it in a quiet plea to let him finish his thought.

"I kinda just sat with it all for the week, you know, the guys at the bar saw the whole thing, people at my work…" he trails off. Silent tears start streaming down my face as I recognize that he doesn't believe that this was all an editing job and he's not here to give me a movie romcom ending. Instead, he's here to say goodbye and tell me what a lunatic I am. I avert my eyes and wipe my face.

"I understand," I say, "and again I'm so incredibly sorry."

He takes his hand it puts it on top of mine and holds it there for a moment, the warmth of the gesture serves to make me start crying once again.

"Maddy came to see me yesterday," he says. His face softens and he is again looking at me directly.

"What?" I question. What the hell has she done? As if she hasn't ruined my life enough.

"You Novak women are apparently excellent stalkers," his tone straddles the line between being jokey and serious. "She came to the bar last night. You should've heard the needle scratch off the record when she walked in. I don't think many of those guys have seen a woman under 25-years-old in person in years, let alone one who looks all made up like Maddy."

"Are you kidding me?" I say angrily. "I swear I haven't talked to her since I told her off at Navy Pier."

"She said as much," he explains. "She seemed broken up about that and basically came to try to convince me to give you a second chance. She confessed that her team had edited the video together to appease that mental health sponsor and make sure that there was enough of a hook to get their viewers to watch. She said that she hadn't seen you be this passionate and smitten about a guy, ever, really. Not even your ex-husband."

Brian's recounting of the conversation is very matter of fact and I can't figure out if it's about to get worse or better.

"Maddy also said that despite the fact that you can be a total mess, you're kind of the coolest person she knows," he recalls. "She apologized to me for what she did and how it may have affected me. She said that she hoped I would consider giving you another shot."

"Wow," I whisper. I find it difficult to believe that Maddy would have done all this. Much like her mother she is extremely anti-confrontational and fairly quick to just cancel people rather listen, explain, and make amends. To be fair, in this situation, making a move as bold as the one that she did would even be way out of my own comfort zone.

"So that's where we are, and that's why I'm here," he says. "To see if I should give you another shot."

I look up at him and he's looking straight into my eyes, with his hand still over my hand. I let his thought and silence hang in the air for a moment, hoping that he quickly reveals his decision. When he doesn't say anything more, I start speaking.

"Well..." I start, "I guess the pros of giving me another shot are that it can only get better from here since I pretty much showed you how being in my orbit can make things hit rock bottom from day one. I think we also have good chemistry, and I've proven that I'm not afraid to tell the world how good you are in bed. I may have a job soon, or may not, but am at least making headway in that realm, so I hopefully won't be a totally unemployed loser for much longer. And I guess another pro, is that I really do like you and think you are a special guy who is none of those boring 'dude' things that that ass-backwards video made it seem like I thought you were."

Brian continues to look at me without breaking eye contact and seems to be attempting to stare into my soul. I feel like I did when I was a teenager and confessed to my father that I'd dented his car while trying to parallel park. He just glued his eyes to me trying to figure out what, if anything, my punishment should be, knowing full well that a few moments sitting through the uncertainty of his stare was punishment enough.

"And the cons?" he asks.

"The cons," I add, "I am not a great cook and I'm pretty bad with money. My family are nutjobs, but they apparently love me more than I realize. Your daughters probably will think you're crazy if you do indeed decide to date me, though I promise if I ever get the pleasure of meeting them, I will suck up to them like no one has ever sucked up to anyone. And, I only own like one pair of sexy underwear and all the rest look like they belong to an 80-year-old-woman, but I do promise that I will devote whatever paycheck that I ultimately get next nearly entirely to lingerie to impress you."

Having laid all my cards on the table, I know that there is nothing more I can say and just hope it is enough to soften his stoic poker face. If he is indeed going to give me a chance, he is most certainly making me work for it.

"You wanna go for a walk?" he asks. "I feel like I'm on meth with all this coffee." Taken aback, but relieved by a potential change in venue, I shake my head yes, still unclear what comes next.

He stands up and throws away his empty coffee cups along with mine. I stand up next to him and start walking to the door.

"Thanks for the coffee, Miles," his voice booms as he waves. "I'll see you first thing tomorrow morning."

Miles waves, and the words take a minute to travel from my ears to my head to my heart. I whip my head up and look at him. Brian winks and grabs my hand as we make our way out to the sidewalk. We meander back to my apartment barely saying a word to each other just leaning in and squeezing each other's hands along the way like a couple that has been through a traumatic event, but still care deeply for each other.

Back at my apartment, we fall into the sofa cuddling limb-to-limb as I infuse the word thank you often and profusely into my musings. We listen to music and talk, and talk, and talk. I learn about his first girlfriend in junior high, the time he broke his leg during a Thanksgiving football game with his brothers, and that one of the few things he can't stand is eating cilantro. He tries hobbies on like most people try on clothes including cheesemaking, beekeeping, and woodworking and that his garage houses the detritus of the hobbies that he chose not to pursue.

I tell him about how my first fender bender was when I ran into the back of a police car in my dad's prized Cutlass Ciera, how the scar on my chin came from crashing into the headboard when I was jumping on my grandmother's bed, and confess that I dislike deep dish pizza and couldn't care less about the Cubs. We share our most embarrassing moments, saddest moments, hopeful moments, and painful details about our divorces in a way that seems like we're cramming two-years' worth of dating into three-hours of conversation. When we finally run out of steam with talking, physical contact takes its place.

"I heard on the internet that I'm pretty good at this," he whispers while removing my shirt.

"Ordinarily I'd say not to believe everything you hear online, but I think in this case it's true. I've been thinking about our night together since the moment you left," I whisper back.

"Well let's see if we can top it," he jokes raising an eyebrow. As our kissing and canoodling starts to get more intimate, my insecurity creeps in.

"Would you mind if we kicked things off with a quick shower?" I ask taking his hand. "I spent the day walking around the city and would love to wash the grime off."

"As long as you don't ask me to adjust your water pressure, and I can choose where to soap you up" he says naughtily, "I'm game."

We step into my standalone shower and proceed to have a soapy and steamy make out session that manages to avoid the pitfalls of every previous tandem shower I've ever tried. No one is left standing in a waterless no-mans-land corner of the shower cold, bored, or waiting their turn for the soap. I'm just struck by how surprisingly easy everything is when I'm with Brian. Even a tandem shower just seems to work.

We step out of the shower, dry off thanks to large fluffy towels Riff provided me, and tumble over to my bed. We continue to explore each other's bodies with abandon to orgasmic results. Afterward we cuddle close to each other, drifting in and out of consciousness awaking multiple times throughout the night to just to touch and feel each other in arousing but not awaking ways.

Brian's phone alarm buzzes at 5 am and we both grumble at the cruelty of it.

"I have to head up to pick up a work van," he kisses my arm.

"Call in sick," I whisper, kissing his neck.

"I wish I could, but we're already down a few people because of vacations," he explains.

"Can I see you again this week?" I mumble with my eyes half open. He's now standing up putting his clothes on.

"I would love that," he says. "Come up to my place

on Thursday night, I'll cook you dinner."

"Yes, please," I agree sleepily sitting up. I stare at him in the hazy darkness. "I'm going to have to meet up with Maddy and thank her," I suddenly acknowledge.

"Well if you do," he says putting his shoes on. "Check that's she not wearing a wire or hidden camera first," he laughs. I throw a pillow in his direction.

I get up and give him a hug and a side mouthed, fearful-that-I-have-morning-breath kiss.

"I'll see you Thursday," I say longingly as he gets ready to step out my door. "And Brian, thank you for the second chance. I won't fuck it up." I smile, and he winks in return.

I return to my bed, sheets twisted and messy, and lay there with my eyes half awake and a smile on my face. I feel hopeful.

I wait two full hours before gathering the courage to send out a text to Debbie and Maddy. Debbie is notorious for refusing to put her phone on do not disturb, as she's paranoid one of the kids may need her at 3 am. The kids have never texted her at that time, but I have been chastised for sending random 2 am can't sleep texts like "Do you remember which flavor of Haagen Dazs ice cream grandma used to keep in her freezer in case fancy people came over?" or "I just realized I'm wearing a blue bra that I have no recollection of buying, is it yours?"

Figuring that 7 am is a reasonable hour, I begin drafting my message.

> Sister Debbie + Maddy: Waving the white flag. You 2 available for a non-fancy lunch today? Grab sandwiches and sit on the riverwalk? 1 pm at the usual spot?

After hitting send, I watch dots appear after Debbie's name nearly immediately. They soon disappear, and knowing Debbie so well, I know that that's her version of "I don't want to look too eager," which puts me at ease. She waits a whole five more minutes before typing again.

> Sister Debbie: We're in. Maddy is still sleeping, she slept over here last night. I hate that I missed you...but I did, bitch.

I react with a heart emoji and am bursting at the seams to talk to her. I fall asleep for a few hours and wake up with just enough time to pull myself together and grab a train downtown. On the L, I look up Maddy's YouTube channel, just to see where everything might stand. There was a new video from two days ago that was simply titled "Reevaluating." I put in my earbuds and watch as Maddy delivers a message from her dining room/

office.

"Hey MadLovers, and I guess I should also say MadHaters, as I know there's been a lot of both on my channel over the last week. First off, I want to say I'm sorry. I'm sorry to anyone who has been offended by anything I may have done or said. My life is a journey and this has definitely been a learning experience for me. As I continue on this journey of authenticity, self-acceptance, and self-actualization, I would hope that you all can find it in your hearts to offer me some grace." A tear starts to fall out of Maddy's perfectly made-up eye, as if she had studied the Sinead O'Connor "Nothing Compares 2 U" video and was trying to reenact it wearing false lashes and extensions. "I'm in a period of transition right now and am taking a few weeks off from my grueling schedule to recenter, reprioritize, and truly figure out what's next for me and my channel. This is a time of growth for me and I'm excited to see what the future brings. I also want to take a minute to apologize to Jackie. I'm not sure if she'll ever see this, but I do want her to know I'm sorry. So with that, I'm signing off for now, but wishing you all MadLove through the good and bad times." She blows a kiss at the camera and it goes dark.

The comments on the video range from appropriate, to supportive, to deranged, to irrelevant. I once again wonder why a young woman would do this to herself, but given that her subscriber numbers were still upwards of a million, I think the ultimate answer is money.

Pleased that both Debbie and Maddy seem to be in a better headspace than when we last interacted, and knowing that I certainly am, I am excited to see them when I walk across the street by the river.

"I missed you guys," I confess with my arms held wide open. They both come in for a hug, Maddy being careful not to rub her face full of makeup on my clothes.

"Part of me is still furious at you," Debbie says, "but I think we can all agree that the situation pushed everyone over the edge." I resist the urge to stir the pot in any way or get defensive or offensive.

"I saw Brian last night," I direct my conversation at Maddy. "He told me what you did. Thank you." She smiles back at me and looks over at her mother.

"That bar he hangs out at is sketch," she mumbles. "It's all old people who seem like they haven't left those bar stools since the 1980s."

"That's pretty accurate," I agree. "But they're happy, and I think I'm realizing that that's all that matters."

"Are you two…" Debbie trails off.

"He's giving me a second shot," I explain. "And we had a lovely sleep over last night." I can't help that my face breaks into a revealing smile.

"Eww," Maddy grimaces, "I don't wanna know."

Debbie kisses my cheek, "I'm happy for you babe." We grab sandwiches and sit down in an area of benches leading down to the river.

"So what's going on with the channel," I ask Maddy. "I saw the last video you put up."

"I'm just figuring things out and re-evaluating everything, my team, the content, pretty much everything," she says. "I lost some subscribers, but gained a bunch of new ones, so I want to figure out where to take it from here. I think I just got really burned out and sort of lost myself there for a minute."

While she still seems like she's wearing a mask of makeup and is significantly over dressed for eating on a bench, for the first time in a long time talking to her feels like I am actually speaking to the Maddy I've always known and loved. Maybe she truly has gotten burned out and lost the line between public and private life. While it was a tough lesson to learn and bitter pill to swallow, it may have been just what she needed to set her on a more sustainable path.

"I'm proud of you," I wink. "And as much as I think your makeover of me was a complete and utter disaster and failure, I do think you in some way really helped makeover my insides. Like for years, I feel like I was trapped in that Gen X 'Whatever' trope where I just sorta went with the flow, taking whatever came at me, good or bad, and like not really having any goals or passions. Just going along with whatever Dan said or did, doing whatever job because it was there, you know, not really trying. Whether that's what was ingrained in me or out of lack of confidence to really go for anything, who knows. But I saw what you and your team built and how so many of your peers are really trying to follow your passions, that I think it ignited something in me. To go for the guy who has a lust for life, to take more risks and chances in general. So yeah…for I that I thank you. The rest of it, not so much." I wink and Debbie shoots me a look to remind me to try to keep the conversation in a positive direction.

We finish our sandwiches and Maddy grabs the trash and heads up to dispose of it and grab an iced tea. Debbie looks at her walking away and waits until she's out of earshot.

"I talked to Tom," she says. Her face starts to crumple up and get flushed. "About sex."

"Wow," I say with surprise. "And…"

"And we had it," she says bluntly. Her tone is akin to the one someone would use when describing that they tried a new flavor of ice cream or ordered from a new take-out restaurant.

"And?" I ask with anticipation.

"And it was very quick," she chirps embarrassingly. "He was so excited, that, you know, it was quick."

"Aww," I jab. "OK, but you kinda broke the seal. Hopped back on the horse. All those sorta inappropriate metaphors. Now that you're having sex, you can work your way back to good sex." She pauses and her eyes look around like she's seeking guidance on how to tell me something.

"I think I'm pregnant," she finally blurts.

"What?" I spit. "We've only stopped talking for a week, how could you possibly be pregnant? Not to mention you're 48. I mean, I guess you still have eggs, but they are probably very old and scrambled at this point."

"This all happened like three weeks ago, I just didn't tell you," she admits. She looks behind her to make sure Maddy isn't returning. "I started to suspect something around the time of Cam's party when you told me Tom made a comment that Dan would be nuts to have a kid in his fifties. I started to panic when I heard that. Then you were going through your own shit, rambling on about your mind-blowing sex and all that. And I just…I felt dumb."

"Wait," I whisper. "You're not kidding?"

"No, Jackie," she snaps. "Not kidding. I'm 48, had the quickest, least mind-blowing sex in the world for the first time in three years and I think I'm fucking pregnant," she says in a yell-whisper.

"Did you tell Tom? I mean, did you take a test?" I have so many questions. "I mean maybe it's just you shocked the shit out of your cycle or something and in a weird perimenopausal way your body is just fucking around? Have you had sex again since that first time?"

"I took three tests," she says looking around again. "They were all sorta positive, I mean not super positive, but like sorta. And no, I haven't told Tom, and no we haven't had sex again. He's been kind of feeling insecure that it was all so quick, so I'm kinda letting him stew in that embarrassment as an excuse while I panic about this."

"I mean, would you want a kid now?" I ask in an accidentally judgmental tone. "Like a brand-new start-all-over-kid now?" I am dumbfounded.

"I'm 48, I have no idea," she says. "I mean part of me just would love to be the perpetual mom, but part of me is like, am I gonna have a toddler in my fucking 50s?"

"Maddy's coming," I say through my teeth.

"I have a doctor's appointment at the end of the week," she says. "Will you…"

"Absolutely," I finish.

ELEVEN
Five Months Later

Brian and his brother Chris are making their last runs down to the truck to bring in my living room table and a couple of lamps inside.

"I have no idea how you were able to fit all this shit into that tiny studio apartment," Brian yells setting the lamp down on the floor. He downs a bottle of water in three gulps and wipes the sweat from his brow.

"It had really good closet space," I confess.

I look around surrounded by boxes and brown paper for what seems like the umpteenth time in the last year and am proud of myself.

Darlene ultimately came through and put in a good word as part of my job search. As the Associate Manager of Editorial Content at the Art Institute of Chicago, my salary is actually less than my previous job, but the quality-of-life and satisfaction with my work has already improved significantly. Realizing that I was living way above my means, I decided to move out of my overpriced studio in my beloved neighborhood and into a less glamorous, but more affordable option a few neighborhoods north, wedged between my old homestead and Brian's house. He'd hinted that I could consider moving in with him, but I realized that I needed a little time to figure out how to be functional and independent Jackie before I start riding on another man's coattails. I think I scored points with his daughters for not taking him up on his offer to cohabitate so soon, as they have welcomed me with somewhat open, yet still skeptical arms and I am well aware that it may take a long time to truly gain their trust.

"Debbie texted that she just got to my mother's and to brace myself as she's in rare form," I convey.

"Is she feeling better?" he asks. Debbie and Brian have become fast friends given that his homemaking hobbies and abilities align with hers more than mine ever could. They exchange recipes, gardening, tips, and I suspect Jackie-management strategies quite regularly.

"Ya, I think she's doing better," I confirm.

"Well if you're gonna be heading over there, I may go back to Jeff Park with Chris, grab a shower, take care of a few things around the house, and then maybe I can grab you some groceries and make you a late dinner in your new kitchen tonight?" he smiles.

"Aww, babe," I coo. "If that is code for picking up Thai takeout because I have no idea where any of my cookware, pots, pans, plates, or silverware are, then yeah, cool," I laugh.

"Noted," he touches his temple.

"Good luck, Jackie," Chris waves. "New place is cute, great light." He goes downstairs and I hug a very sweaty Brian goodbye despite knowing that I will see him again in a few hours.

"Thank you for all you've done today," I smile and touch his face. "I really appreciate it."

"My pleasure. You deserve this," he rubs my back. I can't help thinking back to my last move when I basically threw my stuff into trash backs and made thirty trips back and forth from apartment to apartment hoping that Dan and I wouldn't have another argument about who originally bought the dishtowels, iron, or something else neither one of actually wanted, but we didn't want to concede to each other. "I'll see you in a bit," Brian adds. "Tell Debbie I say hi and don't let your mother get to you two." I give him a quick kiss and squeeze his hand as he heads out the door.

I change out of my moving clothes and put more thought into what I will wear to my mother's house than I did in choosing what to wear for my first day of work, as my mother's criticism and judgment can cut deeper than any stranger's. I head across town on the bus listening to a podcast that touts that it can bring you into a state of calm. By the time I arrive at my mother's house the only state I am firmly in is one of pure anxiety. I let myself in with the key that I've had since the 1980s.

"Hello family," I say loudly assuming someone somewhere will hear me as I hang up my coat in the front hallway. "How's everyone doing?"

"It's nice that you finally grace us with your presence Jacqueline," my mother snarks from the living room on the other side of the wall. "I mean it's practically time for you to leave." I take a deep breath, square my shoulders, and walk around the corner.

"OK," I say in a sarcastic tone. "I see how today is gonna go." I make sisterly eye contact with Debbie across the room, which she returns with an eye roll so complete I worry that she may injure herself. "I actually spent the morning moving into a new place, mom. So, it's been quite a day."

"All you ever do, Jackie, is move," my mother comments. "Hopefully you won't get kicked out of this place." I can feel my internal temperature rising like it used to when I was a teenager.

"I wasn't kicked out of any place, mother," I sigh. "In each case I moved into better situations." She doesn't respond, but instead looks out the window and raises an eyebrow as if she is telling an invisible friend that I'm a liar.

"I need some tea," Debbie declares. I don't know if she is trying to save my mother from destroying me, me from destroying my mother, or herself from the cumulative passive aggressive abuse she has just been experiencing from the time she's already been there. "Jackie, can you help me make some tea?" She gets up and half pushes me out of the living room toward the kitchen.

Debbie's pregnant belly seems to have grown exponentially since the last time I saw her just a few days ago. Unlike one of those young pregnant women who look like yoga teachers who happen to have swallowed a basketball, Debbie's pregnancy weight looks more like an overall roundness, which has annoyed her to no end. Given her age, those who know her, and those who don't, fail to assume that she's pregnant and instead offer unsolicited diet tips, perimenopause advice, and judgmental looks if she's seen putting anything remotely caloric into her mouth.

"I'm going to strangle her," Debbie whispers when we reach the kitchen. "In the last 15 minutes she's managed to tell me what a big mistake I'm making having another kid and how she almost wonders if she'd have been better off if she hadn't had us!" I respond with a jaw-dropping, scrunched up facial expression.

"Oh, that's fantastic," I shake my head. "Don't let her get to you, Debs. We are doing our daughterly duty of visiting her and making sure she's healthy, isn't living in squalor, and has groceries. We don't get to be her punching bags on top of that."

"Well good luck with that, because I think she's been taking emotional boxing lessons," she replies. "Tom's picking me up in an hour. You can leave with me if you want. I don't think she'll care."

"Done and done," I smile.

"Maddy's been giving me lectures about managing my stress, so I'm limiting my dose of mom in the name of being mindful," she adds.

Both Maddy and Cameron freaked out when Debbie told them she was pregnant, but no one could've expected that it would've inspired Maddy to begin training to become a doula. She became so intent on helping her mother through this new chapter of her life, she began studying and taking courses almost immediately. She plans to help coach Debbie through the birth. Debbie agreed, grateful for the support, however she made Maddy promise that absolutely nothing would be filmed as part of the process, as she doesn't want her vagina to become viral content or the content that precedes a coupon code for vaginal rejuvenation. While Maddy agreed, her MadLove channel and associated outlets have now taken on a maternity slant which has inspired a whole new set of followers.

Meanwhile, determined not to live in a house with a newborn baby, Cameron's reaction took a different turn and he decided to move out to Silicon Valley to join a gaming start up. He lives in a small apartment with six other nerdy college age boys where they sip caffeinated beverages until all hours of the night and morning while they program online avatar adventures.

"Are you two just gonna leave me sitting out here while you gossip? Or are you actually making tea?" my mother yells from the living room.

"One hour," I whisper to Debbie, "we can do this." I open the fridge to get out the milk and in doing so notice that my mother has pinned Dan's baby announcement including a picture of him, Anna, and their newborn, to the fridge with a "Best Grandma" magnet that Maddy made back when she was in elementary school. "What the fuck is this?" I point it out to Debbie.

"I guess Dan having a kid is something to celebrate, but me having one is a huge mistake," she says equally offended as I am. I flip the smiling picture over in my own act of passive aggression and re-stick it to the fridge as we return to the living room.

"Mom, why did you tack up a picture of Dan's new family on the fridge?" I ask in a tone that tries to remain calm. "You do remember we're divorced and he very much hurt me, right?"

"Oh stop being so sensitive, Jackie," she waves me off. "Dan was always so lovely to me. You wouldn't give him a child, so he had to go find someone that would. That's not his fault. I think it's nice that he sent me the announcement. At least someone's thinking of me." I sit there, mouth agape, not sure where even to begin.

"Don't even bother, Jacks," Debbie intervenes. "Mom's in a mood today." When Debbie starts talking about my mother as if she's not sitting mere feet away, you know the situation has turned particularly dire.

"You do know we are your daughters, mom, right? We are here to see you. You can try to be nice to us and pretend you care," I dig. She looks at me for a moment as if thinking of a way to respond.

"Debbie says you have a new job," she changes the topic.

"Ya," I confirm, trying to keep the peace. "It's going really well. It's at the Art Institute. Do you remember Darlene? Who I went to high school with? She put in a good word for me and I'm thrilled to finally be doing something I'm excited about."

"That's good," she acknowledges. "I mean museums don't pay a lot, but I know you are just like your father and always like those museums." I glance over at Debbie, unsure whether to take that comment as a win or loss.

"Oh, speaking of the old days," my mother turns to us animatedly. "I've put together a few boxes of your old stuff up in your rooms. While you're here, go upstairs and look through it and take anything you want. I'm going to throw the rest of it out. I am thinking of redoing your rooms. Maybe a guest room, or a craft room. I've seen so many projects I want to try on YouTube."

"You've been saying that for 25 years, mom," Debbie responds.

"Well, if you would just get rid of your crap, I could make it happen, Deborah," my mother holds steady. Debbie and I look at each other knowing that there's no use arguing with her. My mother hasn't had an out-of-town guest in more than a decade and the last time she attempted to be crafty she ended up at urgent care because she burned herself on a hot glue gun.

"Come on, big mama," I walk over and stick my hand out to help Debbie up. "Let's go sort through the ghosts of our pasts." Both Debbie and I have done this exercise countless times since we moved out when we were college age. We usually throw my mother an olive branch by removing a book or poster or some small token, so it looks like we made an effort to get rid of things, and then we simply push our respective boxes back in the closet so that she can pull it out the next time we come over.

The upstairs of the house is a time capsule to our youth. The wallpaper in the hallway remains unchanged, as do the multi-photo frames that hang on the wall that could aptly be called "the hairstyles we've tried." One cut out circle frame features Debbie's face surrounded by a lion's mane worth of permed hair and the square cut out frame below it shows me standing next to my grandmother sporting a bright red mullet. My old room has been turned into a dumping ground for everything that my mom wants to keep out of sight, but doesn't have the physical or emotional energy to dispose of, including most of my father's old clothes and shoes.

Debbie's old room serves as a shrine to the golden child who she hopes will one day return, despite treating her quite poorly. I grab a box that is on the floor in my old room and bring it into hers as we start sorting through the latest round of treasures, bitching about my mother's attitude and backhanded comments.

"You have to bring those home," I point to a set of rainbow legwarmers that Debbie wore in a junior high school dance recital. "I betcha Maddy would wear those now. And if not, someone she knows most certainly would."

"Only if you bring this home," she pulls a t-shirt out of my box. "Braces make beautiful faces." The shirt has a smiling cartoon girl face where the teeth are covered in silver puffy paint braces. The back of the shirt has the phone number of my teenage orthodontist, Dr. Guski, on it.

"I bet I could donate it in Wicker Park and someone would snap all this up," I laugh.

The boxes are extremely sparse and random seeing as this act of culling down objects is a semi-annual occurrence. Debbie and I surmise that as long as she can blame us having stuff occupying her home, she has an excuse not to move forward and clear out my father's things or update any of the rooms as she claims she wants to do.

"Oh my God," I pull out a large notebook that had doodling all over the cover. "This was my drawing notebook junior year. I haven't seen this thing in like 35 years." I start flipping through the pages which are a combination of bad teenage artwork, notes, and reminders about school, plans with people, and ripped pages that either served as notes passed in class or memories torn and thrown away.

"You used to carry that thing everywhere," she reminisces. "I remember I was so curious, because you used to slam it shut when I would come by. I thought it was like a diary with deep dark secrets about sex and smoking and everything else that I thought you were doing that was taboo at the time."

"Four years was a major age gap back then," I remind her. "I didn't want my little nosy sister looking at my shit." It's funny how age gaps that seem generationally wide when you are a kid disappear over the years. Now when I see a young person on the street, I have no idea if they are 11, 17, or 26. Back when I was a kid, I could decipher someone's age within a 6-month window by just seeing what kind of shoes and haircut they had.

"Well, I did it anyway," she confesses. "I remember sneaking a peak at that one, or maybe it was one from another year, and being super disappointed that it was just pictures and random scribbles that I didn't understand."

"Serves you right, you little snoop," I laugh. I continue thumbing through the first few pages and stop at one scribble. "Look at this," I point out a heart with an arrow through it that says "Jackie -n- Jacque."

"Jacque?" Debbie asks. "Who was that?"

"He was this foreign exchange student from Paris who lived with the Edmunds for junior year," I reply. "I was obsessed with him, because he smoked roll-up cigarettes, wore stripey tops, and seemed so exotic. I don't even think I said more than a few words to him the whole year, but that may just be because he didn't speak English all that well."

"Freak," she laughs and nudges me with her foot.

"We should go back down there before mom gets pissed that we have to leave."

"Do you think she's losing her mind?" I ask sincerely. "Like not in a funny, everyone thinks their parents are nuts, she's losing her mind kinda way. But you know in a scary, sad, real dementia sorta way? I mean she's always been harsh, and always has ridden me hard, but she seems even more angry than usual and seems to be ripping you a new one too. She never used to do that."

"I honestly don't know, Jack," Debbie throws up her arms. "Maybe it's age, loneliness, or just no longer giving a fuck so even the little bit of censor that she used to have is completely gone. I mean she seems independent still. The house is clean, she claims to go out with friends, and she is still getting around pretty well."

"I think she watches too much TV," I say.

"That could be part of it," Debbie agrees. She starts to roll toward her side to get traction to get up again and I once again offer a hand. "My back is killing me, but not because of the baby. Tom and I keep trying new sexual positions to see what feels best at the moment and I think he made me pull a muscle last night."

"Deborah Marie," I fake clutching my pearls, "you filthy whore." I laugh and make lude high school-level sexual gestures.

"I should've known better than to bring it up,"

she says regretfully. "It's just my hormones have turned me into a raging sex machine and Tom is on this health kick to make sure he's not a decrepit old dad. He's running all the time so he's all jazzed up too. So it's like we've gotten our second wind in that department."

"Aww," I tuck the notebook under my arm as we walk down the hallway. "I'm happy for you guys." Debbie smiles and for the first time in a long time seems genuinely happy for herself too.

When we return to the living room, my mother has already removed our mugs of tea and put the throw pillows on the couch back to their starting position, as a subliminal signal that she's ready for us to leave so she can go back to business as usual in her home. That's been the general theme with her since we were kids. She likes the idea of us, so she can tell friends, family, and strangers about her wonderful two daughters, but in practice she finds us annoying, troublesome, and generally an inconvenience that makes her life rather untidy. She'll put on the show of saying we don't visit enough, but when we do, she insults us and makes us wonder why we came. It's a dance we do, because that's what this obligation called family has turned into with her and we know our father would've wanted us to.

"That's all you're taking?" she asks, pointing at the few things in our arms. "Are you sure? I'm going to throw the rest of it out. I'm thinking of starting an Etsy business and will need the room to make things to sell. I'm gonna have my third act as the next Martha Stewart." I think back to the sad Halloween costumes and gloppy papier mâché Christmas ornaments she tried to make every year and raise an eyebrow to acknowledge that Martha Stewart has nothing to worry about.

"Yup, all good mom," Debbie confirms. "We're getting things ready for another baby, so I've just been downsizing things lately, I don't need to add any more crap to the pile."

"Suit yourself," she responds, clearly hoping we don't sit back down.

"Tom is coming to pick us up in a few," Debbie offers. "So I'm just going to pee one more time before we head out."

"In and out with you two," my mother says, clearly relieved.

"You should come out and see my new apartment sometime, mom," I say half-heartedly. "It's only a bus ride across town, or I can send a cab for you."

"You never live in very nice neighborhoods, Jacqueline," my mother comments. "I think I prefer to stay on this side of town."

"Right," I turn my back, roll my eyes, and start gathering my things. When I turn back around with my coat on, my mother is standing mere inches from me.

"You know that I love you, Jackie," she says sincerely. "Right? I mean I'm not sure if you love me, but I love you."

"Geez, mom," I startle. "Yes, of course. I love you, even if you are a proper pain in the ass most of the time." I hug her and she seems smaller and older than just a few moments ago.

I marvel at her ability to use her words to make me feel like a worthless, insignificant little girl in one moment and in the next make me feel like I'm somehow the heartless instigator of our strained relationship. I learned long ago to keep my guard up as high as a maximum-security prison fence when I'm around her. I divulge only information that I feel I can handle being poked at with a stick and it not do permanent damage. As such, she will only learn of the existence of Brian once I feel good and ready and that it has established roots to withstand my mother blowing hurricane force winds at it. For years this made me feel incredibly guilty, like I was hiding my life from the one person who is supposed to love me unconditionally. Through years of therapy and self-discovery, I've learned that the only way to protect my heart and mind with her is solid boundaries and a healthy dose of humor.

"Oh boy," Debbie exclaims, "I'm in the bathroom for two minutes and you two are hugging. Is the world ending?"

"I don't know how I raised such sarcastic daughters," my mother shakes her head and helps Debbie put her coat on. "I blame your father. Those sharp tongues didn't come from me, that's all him."

"Bye mom," I say, knowing she has the sharpest tongue of all. "We'll see you soon." Debbie and I walk outside and feel an immediate sense of relief the moment we hear the door close behind us.

"We're free," Debbie whispers without moving her mouth in case our mother is still watching us from the front window behind the sheer curtains.

"Let's walk down the block a little bit to wait for Tom so that she can't spy on us so easily," I suggest, a strategy that I implemented as a teenager in hopes that my mother wouldn't catch me smoking cigarettes while I waited for a friend to pick me up.

"She won't be around forever," Debbie states the obvious.

"Yes she will," I respond. "Her voice is what my therapist calls self-doubt and insecurity," I laugh. "She'll be with me forevermore."

We see Tom pull around and wave, point, and indicate with fifteen different hand gestures that he was going to drive around the block and come meet us going the other direction.

"I know she'll never say it," Debbie says, "so I will just so you hear it. You're amazing, Jackie. You've embarked on this next chapter of your life like a fucking champ and I'm so proud of you and optimistic for your future."

"Aww Debs," I say caught off guard with tears in my eyes. "Back atcha my hero sister. You have been more of a mom to me over these last few months than mom ever was. And you are going to give kiddo three the best damn life."

Debbie reacts with near sobs as her hormone levels have turned her into an emotional pool. Tom pulls up and jumps out of the car.

"What did Maggie say?" he asks earnestly, seeing her well up. "Did she insult you again? I know she's your mother, but goddamn, you don't have to withstand this abuse." Debbie waves him off.

"No," I correct. "Surprisingly it was me complimenting her that set off these waterworks," I nudge. Tom puts his hand on Debbie's back. "You're looking like a regular Clark Kent mixed with a jock!" I jab at Tom's side.

"Thanks," he smiles proudly. "Up to six miles a day even in bad weather," he pats his now toned ab area. "Gotta make sure I'm ready for this kid and can fit in with the other dads. It was either turn into a fitness freak or start dying my hair and master the art of TikTok. Running seemed like the easier option." Debbie starts to go toward the passenger side of the car.

"I'm just gonna take the bus," I start to back up. "I

want to go down memory lane with my old doodle book for a while and process the latest interaction with mom surrounded by 20 or so complete strangers.

"You sure?" Debbie asks. Debbie's days of takings public transit ended about twenty years ago when she was coming to visit Tom and I and ended up sitting in a puddle of urine that she hadn't seen on the seat.

"Ya," I say. "I'll see you guys in two weeks for brunch with Brian, right?" Tom nods and gives me a hug.

As they pull away, Tom gives me the requisite double honk as he heads northward and I proceed to wait at the bus stop a few blocks away.

Settling into my bus seat, I pull out the doodle notebook and leaf through the later pages. Cartoon characters that I used to draw litter the pages interspersed with nonsense, words, phone numbers, times, names of books, concert dates, and abstract shapes and lines. The notebook had manilla pockets on either end of it, which were perfect for storing notes, cash, or even an old joint or two. In this one I found an old chemistry test which I'd gotten a failing grade on which I'd likely shoved in the pocket to hide from my mother who often took it upon herself to snoop through all my stuff like a prison guard searching a cell for contraband.

Behind the test was a sealed envelope that I'd never seen before. I pull it out and immediately lose my breath at the sight of my father's handwriting as I hadn't seen my name written by him in over a decade. On the front it says "Jackie Age 17." I feverishly open it.

Inside is a piece of stationary that has "From the Desk of Jack Novak" printed on top. Below it is a hand written letter with my father's printed scrawl across it.

Dear Jackie,

As you go off to your senior year of high school, I thought I'd give you a little time capsule of advice of sorts so that if you are reading this at some point – assuming your mother doesn't find it and throw it out first – you can remember where you came from.

My darling girl, my first born, my namesake, you are fierce, stubborn and a force to be reckoned with. Remember though, not everything has to be a reckoning. You will get what you want and deserve, even it takes longer than you would like to do so.

As close as you are with your friends, remember there is no one quite like family and even though you might think she's a little snot right now, cherish Debbie as you two are destined to be two peas in a pod.

Shake that world up, no matter what anyone says, including your mom. She sees in you what she always wanted to be. Even though she may not always show it, you make her proud. And you make me very proud too, even if you sometimes do dumb shit.

Love you to the moon and stars and back, my little redheaded one.

Jack Novak

Tears stream down my face as I rack my brain as to why I'm just finding this letter now. I suppose that may have been by design, in that my father hid it in a notebook that he knew I would likely abandon at the end of the school year. My tears are punctuated by a fit of laughter as I realize that he signed it using his full name, as if dad wouldn't have been formal enough. I tuck the letter back in the envelope and put it in the pocket of the notebook before my neighboring bus passengers label me the crazy lady having a public meltdown on the bus.

Four stops later, I get off in front of my new home. I walk upstairs into the small but bright space, slightly overwhelmed by the day's activity and very overwhelmed by the task of unpacking what awaits me. I set the notebook down and pull out my phone to discover a new text from Brian.

> Brian: Hope you and Debbie survived the day at your mom's. Still up for me bringing dinner over? 7:30ish work?
>
> Me: She was in rare form, but my father saved the day at the end (I'll explain later). Very much looking forward to tonight. 7:30 is perfect – hopefully will find the plates by then.

Unsure of where to even begin unpacking I start poking through boxes, pulling out sheets and towels so that at the very least I can make up the bed and take a shower at some point. It's unclear why I didn't label the boxes in any way, but as my father so eloquently put it, I guess I just sometimes do dumb shit.

Wrapped within the set of sheets, which were used as makeshift bubble wrap and padding, I unearth my record player and set it up on a side table. The larger square box in the corner is a dead giveaway for my record collection, which I hope has survived yet another move. I cut the box open and feel my hands skimming through the record spines like they are a Ouija board Planchette, searching to reveal the exact musical interlude for this moment. Within moments I land on *(What's the Story) Morning Glory?* By Oasis.

The bulk of my life may have been spent searching for something unknown, but settling for "whatever" came my way. However, looking around at what I've accomplished, who I'm surrounded by, and where I am now, I know that it took a lifetime of "whatevers" to get me where I am today. And today I am, I dare say, happy.

I put the record on the mat, start the turntable and drop the needle on "Don't Look Back in Anger." Thoroughly satisfied, I smile as the first notes play.

ACKNOWLEDGEMENTS

A heartfelt thank you to everyone who encouraged me—or at least resisted the urge to raise an eyebrow—when I shared my plans to write romantic fiction. And to those who couldn't resist (looking at you, Tina), thank you for keeping me grounded by pointing out that this *had* to be fiction, given my famously terrible flirting skills. You weren't wrong!

Most importantly, my deepest gratitude goes to my real-life leading man, Eric Hauser, for his invaluable editing, unwavering support, and for being my very own happily ever after.

ABOUT THE AUTHOR

***

Jen LiMarzi grew up in New York with a big imagination and a love for spinning stories. By day, she's spent years as a medical communicator writing about scientific breakthroughs and managing diseases. By night,  she's inherently a humorist, with her essays appearing in magazines, online outlets, and in collections.

A lifelong fan of rom-coms, meet-cutes, and happy endings, Jen's taken the plunge into romantic fiction. She currently lives in Chicago with her husband, Eric, and their melodramatic dog, Astro. (www.JenLiMarzi.com)

Made in the USA
Monee, IL
11 January 2025

76629224R00173